The Clue

Carolyn Wells

The Clue

ISBN: 978-1-63637-839-8

CONTENTS

CONTENTS

I

THE VAN NORMANS

The old Van Norman mansion was the finest house in Mapleton. Well back from the road, it sat proudly among its finely kept lawns and gardens, as if with a dignified sense of its own importance, and its white, Colonial columns gleamed through the trees, like sentinels guarding the entrance to the stately hall.

All Mapleton was proud of the picturesque old place, and it was shown to visiting strangers with the same pride that the native villagers pointed out the Memorial Library and the new church.

More than a half-century old, the patrician white house seemed to glance coldly on the upstart cottages, whose inadequate pillars supported beetling second stories, and whose spacious, filigreed verandas left wofully small area for rooms inside the house.

The Van Norman mansion was not like that. It was a long rectangle, and each of its four stories was a series of commodious, well-shaped apartments.

And its owner, the beautiful Madeleine Van Norman, was the most envied as well as the most admired young woman in the town.

Magnificent Madeleine, as she was sometimes called, was of the haughty, imperious type which inspires admiration and respect rather than love. An orphan and an heiress, she had lived all of her twenty-two years of life in the old house, and since the death of her uncle, two years before, had continued as mistress of the place, ably assisted by a pleasant, motherly chaperon, a clever social secretary, and a corps of capable servants.

The mansion itself and an income amply sufficient to maintain it were already legally her own, but by the terms of her uncle's will she was soon to come into possession of the bulk of the great fortune he had left.

Madeleine was the only living descendant of old Richard Van Norman, save for one distant cousin, a young man of a scapegrace and ne'er-do-weel sort, who of late years had lived abroad.

This young man's early life had been spent in Mapleton, but, his fiery temper having brought about a serious quarrel with his uncle, he had wisely concluded to take himself out of the way.

And yet Tom Willard was not of a quarrelsome disposition. His bad temper was of the impulsive sort, roused suddenly, and as quickly suppressed. Nor was it often in evidence. Good-natured,

1

easy-going Tom would put up with his uncle's criticism and fault-finding for weeks at a time, and then, perhaps goaded beyond endurance, he would fly into a rage and express himself in fluent if rather vigorous English.

For Richard Van Norman had been by no means an easy man to live with. And it was Tom's general amiability that had made him the usual scapegoat for his uncle's ill temper. Miss Madeleine would have none of it. Quite as dictatorial as the old man himself she allowed no interference with her own plans and no criticism of her own actions.

This had proved the right way to manage Mr. Van Norman, and he had always acceded to Madeleine's requests or submitted to her decrees without objection, though there had never been any demonstration of affection between the two.

But demonstration was quite foreign to the nature of both uncle and niece, and in truth they were really fond of each other in their quiet, reserved way. Tom Willard was different. His affection was of the honest and outspoken sort, and he made friends easily, though he often lost them with equal rapidity.

On account, then, of his devotion to Madeleine, and his enmity toward young Tom Willard, Richard Van Norman had willed the old place to his niece, and had further directed that the whole of his large fortune should be unrestrictedly bestowed upon her on her wedding-day, or on her twenty-third birthday, should she reach that age unmarried. In event of her death before her marriage, and also before her twenty-third birthday, the whole estate would go to Tom Willard.

It was with the greatest reluctance that Richard Van Norman decreed this, but a provision had to be made in case of Madeleine's early death, and Willard was the only other natural heir. And now, at twenty-two, Madeleine was on the eve of marriage to Schuyler Carleton, a member of one of the oldest and best families of Mapleton.

The village gossips were pleased to commend this union, as Mr. Carleton was a man of irreproachable habits, and handsome enough to appear well beside the magnificent Madeleine.

He was not a rich man, but, as her marriage would bring her inheritance, they could rank among the millionaires of the day. Yet there were those who feared for the future happiness of this apparently ideal couple.

Mrs. Markham, who was both housekeeper and chaperon to her young charge, mourned in secret over the attitude of the betrothed pair.

2

"He adores her, I'm sure," she said to herself, "but he is too courtly and polished in his manner. I'd rather he would impulsively caress her, or involuntarily call her by some endearing name than to be always so exquisitely deferential and polite. And Madeleine must love him, or why should she marry him? Yet she is so haughty and formal, she might be a very duchess instead of a young American girl. But that's Madeleine all over. I've never seen her exhibit any real emotion over anything. Ah, well, I'm an old-fashioned fool. Doubtless, they're cooing doves when alone together, but their high-bred notions won't allow any sentiment shown before other people. But I almost wish she were going to marry Tom. He has sentiment and enthusiasm enough for two, and the relationship is so distant it's not worth thinking about. Dear old Tom! He's the only one who ever stirs Madeleine out of that dignified calm of hers."

And that was true enough. Madeleine had inherited the Van Norman traits of dignity and reserve to such an extent that it was difficult for any one to be a really close friend.

She had, too, a strange little air of preoccupation, and even when interested in a conversation would appear to look through or beyond her companion in a way that was discouraging to the average caller.

So Miss Van Norman was by no means a favorite with the Mapleton young people in a personal sense, but socially she was their leader, and to be on her invitation list was the highest aspiration of the village "climbers."

And now that she was about to marry Schuyler Carleton, the event of the wedding was the only thing talked of, thought of, or dreamed of by Mapleton society.

Madeleine, who always kept in touch with Tom Willard by correspondence, had written him of her approaching marriage, and he had responded by coming at once to America to attend the ceremony.

Relieved from the embarrassment of his uncle's presence, Tom was his jovial self, and showed forth all the reprehensible attractiveness which so often belongs to the scapegrace nature. He sometimes quarreled with Madeleine over trifles, then, making up the next minute, he would caress and pet her with the privileged air of a relative.

He was glad to be back among the familiar scenes of Mapleton, and he went about the town renewing old acquaintances and making new ones, and charming all by his winning personality.

In less than a week he had more friends in the village than Schuyler Carleton had ever made.

3

Carleton, though handsome and distinguished-looking, was absolutely without personal magnetism or charm, which traits were found in abundance in Tom Willard.

The friends of Schuyler Carleton attributed his reserved, almost repellent demeanor to shyness, and this was partly true. His acquaintances said it was indifference, and this again, was partly true. Then his enemies, of whom he had some, vowed that his cold, curt manner of speech was merely snobbishness, and this was not true at all.

His manner toward his fiancée was all that the most exacting could require in the matter of courtesy and punctilious politeness. He was markedly undemonstrative in public, and if this were true of his behavior when the two were alone, it was probably because Madeleine herself neither inspired nor desired terms or acts of endearment.

Tom's attitude toward Madeleine angered Carleton extremely, but when he spoke to her on the subject he was gaily informed that the matter of cousinly affection was outside the jurisdiction of a fiancée.

Tom, on his part, was desperately in love with Madeleine, and had been for years. Repeatedly he had begged her to marry him, and she knew in her heart that his plea was prompted by his love for herself and not by any consideration of her fortune.

And yet, should she marry another, all hope of his uncle's money would be forever lost to Tom Willard.

But prodigal and spendthrift that he was, if Tom felt any regret at his vanishing fortunes, he showed no sign of it. Save for sudden and often easily provoked bursts of temper, he was infectiously gay and merry, and was the life of the house party already gathered under Madeleine's roof.

The fact that Tom was staying at the Van Norman house, which of course Carleton could not do, gave Willard an advantage over the prospective bridegroom, of which he was by no means unconscious. Partly to tease the imperturbable but jealous Carleton, and partly because of his own affection for his cousin, Tom devoted himself assiduously to Madeleine, especially when Carleton was present.

"You see, Maddy," Tom would say, "there are only a few days left of our boy and girl chumminess. I fancy that after you are married, Schuyler won't let me speak to you, save in most formal terms, so I must see all I can of you now."

Then he would tuck her arm through his own, and take her for a stroll in the grounds, and Carleton, coming to search for her, would

4

find them cosily chatting in a secluded arbor, or drifting lazily in a canoe on the tiny, lily-padded lake.

These things greatly annoyed Schuyler Carleton, but remonstrance was never an easy task for him, nor did it ever affect Madeleine pleasantly.

"I wish, Madeleine," he had said one day, when he had waited two hours for her to return from a drive with Tom, "that you would have a little regard for appearances, if you have none for my wishes. It is not seemly for my betrothed wife to be driving all over the country with another man."

Magnificent Madeleine looked straight at him, tilting her head back slightly to look beneath her half-closed lids.

"It is not seemly," she said, "for my betrothed husband to imply that I could be at fault in a matter of propriety or punctilio. That is not possible."

"You are right," he said, and his eyes gleamed with admiration of her glorious beauty and imperious manner. "Forgive me,—you are indeed right."

Though Schuyler Carleton may not have been lavish of affection, he begrudged no admiration to the splendid woman he had won.

And yet, had he but known it, the apparently scornful and haughty girl was craving a more tender and gentle love, and would gladly have foregone his admiration to have received more affection.

"But it will come," Madeleine thought to herself. "I am not of the 'clinging vine' type, I know; but after we are married, surely Schuyler will be less formally polite, and more,—well,—chummy."

Yet Madeleine herself was chummy with nobody save Tom.

They two were always chatting and laughing together, and though they differed sometimes, and even quarrelled, it was quickly made up, and forgotten in a new subject of merry discussion.

But, after all, they rarely quarrelled except regarding Madeleine's approaching marriage.

"Don't throw yourself away on that iceberg, Maddy," Tom would plead. "He's a truly fine man, I know, but he can't make you happy."

"How absurd you are, Tom! Give me credit, please, for knowing my own mind, at least. I love Schuyler Carleton, and I am proud that he is to be my husband. He is the finest man I have ever known in every way, and I am a fortunate girl to be chosen by such a man."

"Oho, Maddy! Don't do the humble; it doesn't suit you at all. You are the type who ought to have 'kings and crown princes at your feet.' And Carleton is princely enough in his effects, but he's by no means at your feet."

"What do you mean?" exclaimed Madeleine angrily.

"Just what I say. Schuyler Carleton admires you greatly, but he doesn't love you—at least, not as I do!"

"Don't be foolish, Tom. Naturally you know nothing about Mr. Carleton's affection for me—he does not proclaim it from the housetops. And I desire you not to speak of it again."

"Why should I speak of what doesn't exist? Forgive me, Maddy, but I love you so myself, it drives me frantic to see that man treating you so coolly."

"He doesn't treat me coolly. Or, if he does, it's because I don't wish for tender demonstrations before other people. I'm fond of you, Tom, as you know, but I won't allow even you to criticise the man I am about to marry."

"Oh, very well, marry him, then, and a precious unhappy life you'll lead with him,—and I know why."

Madeleine turned on him, her eyes blazing with anger.

"What do you mean? Explain that last remark of yours."

"Small need! You know why as well as I do;" and Tom pushed his hands into his pockets and strode away, whistling, well knowing that he had roused his cousin's even temper at last.

In addition to some of her Mapleton friends, Madeleine had invited two girls from New York to be her bridesmaids. Kitty French and Molly Gardner had already come and were staying at the Van Norman house the few days that would intervene before the wedding.

Knowing Madeleine well, as they did, they had not expected confidence from her, nor did they look forward to cosy, romantic boudoir chats, such as many girls would enjoy.

But neither had they expected the peculiar constraint that seemed to hang over all the members of the household.

Mrs. Markham had been so long housekeeper, and even companion, for Madeleine that she was not looked upon as a servant, and to her Kitty French put a few discreet questions regarding the exceeding reserve of Mr. Carleton.

"I don't know, Miss French," said the good woman, looking sadly disturbed. "I love Madeleine as I would my own child. I know she adores Mr. Carleton,—and—yes, I know he greatly admires her,—and yet there is something wrong. I can't express it—it's merely a feeling,—an intuition, but there is something wrong."

"You know Mr. Willard is in love with Maddy," suggested Miss French.

"Oh, it isn't that. They've always had a cousinly affection for each other, and,—yes, Tom is in love with her,—but what I mean is aside from all that. The real reason that Madeleine flirts with Tom—for she does flirt with him—is to pique Mr. Carleton. There! I've said more than I meant to, but you're too good a friend to let it make any trouble, and, any way, in a few days they will be married, and then I'm sure it will be all right,—I'm sure of it."

Like many people, Mrs. Markham emphasized by repetition a statement of whose truth she was far from sure.

II

MISS MORTON ARRIVES

The day before the wedding the old house was a pleasant scene of bustle and confusion.

Professional decorators were in charge of the great drawing-room, building a canopy of green vines and flowers, beneath which the bridal pair should stand the next day at high noon.

This work was greatly hindered by a bevy of young people who thought they were helping.

At last, noting a look of dumb exasperation on the face of one of the florist's men, Molly Gardner exclaimed, "I don't believe our help is needed here; come on, Kitty, let's go in the library and wait for tea-time."

It was nearly five o'clock, and the girls found most of the house guests already assembled in the library, awaiting the arrival of the tea-tray.

Several other young people were there also, most of them being those who were to be of the wedding cortège next day.

Robert Fessenden, who was to be best man, had just come from New York, and had dropped in to see Miss Van Norman.

Although he was an old friend of Carleton's, Madeleine did not know him very well, and though she made him welcome, it was with that coldly formal air that did not greatly attract the young man, but he could not fail to be impressed by her great beauty.

"Lucky fellow, Carleton," he said to Tom Willard. "Why, that woman would create a sensation in any great city in the world."

"Yes, she is too handsome to live all her life in a small village," agreed Tom. "I think they intend to travel a great deal."

"An heiress, too, I believe."

"Yes, she has all the desirable traits a woman can possess."

"All?" Fessenden's tone was quizzical.

"What do you mean?" asked Tom sharply.

"Nothing; only, if I were to marry, I should prefer a little more softness of nature."

"Oh, that's only her manner. My cousin is most sweet and womanly, I assure you."

"I'm sure she is," returned Fessenden, who was a bit ashamed of his outspokenness; "and she's getting a sterling good fellow for a husband."

8

"She is so," said Tom, heartily, which was kind of him, considering his own opinion of Carleton.

And then both men strolled over to where Madeleine sat at the tea-table. She was reading a telegram that had just been brought to her, and she laughingly explained to Tom that it meant a bother for him.

"Miss Morton has concluded to come to the wedding, after all," she said. "She wrote me that she wouldn't come, but she has changed her mind, it seems. Now, it does sound ridiculous, I know, but in this big house there isn't a room left for her but the one you have, Tom. You see, one bedroom is used for a 'present room,' one is reserved for Schuyler to-morrow, the bridesmaids have another, and except for our own rooms, and those already occupied by guests, there are no more. I hate to ask you, Tom, but could you go to the Inn?"

"Sure, Maddy dear; anything to oblige. But it does seem too bad to turn me out of your house the very last day that your hospitality is all your own to offer. To-morrow the grand Seigneur will be master here, and my timid little Madeleine can no longer call her soul her own."

This reference to the tall and stately mistress of the house raised a general laugh, but Madeleine did not join in it.

"I'm so sorry, Tom," she said earnestly, as she looked again at the telegram she was holding, "but Miss Morton was an old friend of Uncle Richard's, and as she wants to come here I can't turn her away. And unless you give her your room, there is no other——"

"Nonsense, Madeleine! I'm only joking. Of course I'll go to the hotel. Only too glad to accommodate Miss Morton. Forget it, girl; I assure you I don't mind a bit. I'll pack up a few traps after dinner and skip down to the picturesque, if rather ostentatious, Mapleton Inn."

As Tom spoke he put his arm carelessly round Madeleine's shoulders, and though scarcely more than a cousinly caress, it was unfortunate that Schuyler Carleton should enter the room at that moment. A lightning glance flashed between the two men, and as Tom moved away from Madeleine with a slightly embarrassed shrug of his shoulders, Carleton's face grew so stern that an uncomfortable silence fell upon the guests.

However, the arrival of the tea-tray saved the situation, and Madeleine at once busied herself in the pretty occupation of serving tea to her guests.

With an air of jealous proprietorship, Carleton moved toward her and, looking handsome, though sulky, stood by Willard with folded arms, as if on guard.

9

Urged on by a daredevil spirit of mischief, and perhaps remembering that Madeleine would soon be beyond his reach as Carleton's wife, Tom also moved toward her from the other side. Endeavoring to treat the situation lightly, Madeleine held up a newly-filled teacup.

"Who will have this?" she asked gaily.

"I will!" declared Carleton and Tom at the same time, and each held out a hand.

Madeleine looked at them both smilingly.

Carleton's face was white and set; he was evidently making a serious matter of the trifling episode.

Tom, on the contrary, was smiling broadly, and was quite evidently enjoying his rival's discomfiture.

"I shall give it to you, because you look so pleasant," declared Madeleine, handing the cup to Tom. "Now, Schuyler, smile prettily and you may have one, too."

But Carleton would not fall in with her light mood.

Bending a little, he said in a tense voice, "I will leave you to your cousin now. To-morrow I shall assert my claim."

Though not rude in themselves, the words were accompanied by a harsh and disdainful glance that made several of the onlookers wonder what sort of a life the haughty Madeleine would lead with such a coldly tyrannical husband.

"The brute!" said Tom, under his breath, as Carleton left the room. "Never mind, Maddy, the old Turk has left you to me for this evening, and we'll take him at his word."

Suddenly Madeleine's mood changed to one of utter gaiety. She smiled impartially on all, she jested with the girls, she bewitched the young men with her merry banter, and she almost seemed to be flirting with Tom Willard. But he was her cousin, after all, and much is forgiven a bride-to-be on her wedding eve.

Robert Fessenden looked at Miss Van Norman with a puzzled air. He couldn't seem to understand her, and was glad when by chance the two were left comparatively alone for a few moments' conversation.

"A great responsibility devolves on the best man, Miss Van Norman," he said, in response to a chaffing remark of hers. "I suppose that to-morrow I shall be general director-in-chief, and if anything should go wrong, I shall be blamed."

"But nothing will go wrong," said Madeleine, gaily, "and then, think how you'll be praised!"

"Ah, but you won't be here to hear the praise heaped upon me, so what's the use?"

"No, I shall be gone forever," said Madeleine, putting on one of her faraway looks. "I never want to come back to Mapleton. I hate it!"

"Why, Miss Van Norman! You want to desert this beautiful old house? Schuyler can never find you a home so comfortable and attractive in every way."

"I don't care. I want to go far away from Mapleton to live. We're going to travel for a year, any way, but when we do settle down, it will be abroad, I hope."

"You surprise me. Schuyler didn't tell me this. We've been chums so long, that I usually know of his plans. But, of course, getting married changes all that."

"You're a very intimate friend of Mr. Carleton's, aren't you?" said Madeleine, with a strange note of wistfulness in her voice.

"Yes, I am. Why?"

"Oh, nothing; I only thought—I mean, do you think——"

Rob Fessenden was thrilled by the plaintive expression on the beautiful face, and suddenly felt a great desire to help this girl, who was seemingly so far above and beyond all need of help, and yet was surely about to ask his aid, or at least his sympathy.

"Don't hesitate," he said gently; "what is it, Miss Van Norman? I want to be as firm a friend of yours as I am of Schuyler's, so please say what you wish to."

"I can't—I can't," Madeleine whispered, and her voice was almost a moan.

"Please," again urged Fessenden.

"Do you know Dorothy Burt?" Madeleine then broke out, as if the words were fairly forced from her.

"No," said Fessenden, amazed; "I never heard the name before. Who is she?"

"Hush! She's nobody—less than nobody. Don't mention her to me ever again—nor to any one else. Ah, here comes Miss Morton."

As Fessenden watched Madeleine, she changed swiftly from a perturbed, troubled girl to a courteous, polished hostess.

"My dear Miss Morton," she said, advancing to meet her newest guest, "how kind of you to come to me at this time."

"I didn't come exactly out of kindness," said Miss Morton, "but because I desired to come. I hope you are quite well. Will you give me some tea?"

Miss Morton was a tall, angular lady, with gray hair and sharp, black eyes. She seemed to bite off her words at the ends of her short sentences, and had a brisk, alert manner that was, in a way, aggressive.

"An eccentric," Rob Fessenden thought, as he looked at her, and wondered why she was there at all.

11

"An old sweetheart of Mr. Richard Van Norman, I believe," said Kitty French, when he questioned her. "They were once engaged and then quarrelled and broke it off, and neither of them lived happily ever after."

"As the Carletons will," said Fessenden, smiling.

"Yes," said Kitty slowly, "as the Carletons will—I hope. You know Mr. Carleton awfully well, don't you? Are you sure he will make our Maddy happy, Mr. Fessenden?"

"I think so;" and Fessenden tried to speak casually. "He is not an emotional man, or one greatly given to sentiment, but I judge she is not that sort either."

"Oh, yes, she is! Maddy is apparently cold and cynical, but she isn't really so a bit. But she perfectly adores him, and if they're not happy, it won't be her fault."

"Nor will it be his," said Fessenden, warmly defending his absent friend. "Carleton's an old trump. There's no finer man in the world, and any woman ought to be happy with him."

"I'm glad to hear you say that," said Kitty, with a little sigh of relief. "Do look at that funny Miss Morton! She seems to be scolding Madeleine. I'm sorry she came. She doesn't seem very attractive. But perhaps it's because she was crossed in love and it made her queer."

"Or she was queered in love and it made her cross," laughed Fessenden. "Well, I must go, now, and look up Carleton. Poor old boy, he was a little miffed when he went away."

After tea all the callers departed, and those who were house guests went to their rooms to dress for dinner.

Tom Willard, with great show of burlesque regret and tearful farewells, went to the hotel, that Miss Morton might have the room he had been occupying.

He promised to return for dinner, and gaily blew kisses to Madeleine as with his traps he was driven down the avenue.

At dinner, Schuyler Carleton's place was vacant. It had been arranged next to Madeleine's, and when fifteen minutes after the dinner hour he had not arrived, she haughtily accepted Tom Willard's arm and led the way to the dining-room.

But having reached the table, she directed Tom to take his rightful seat, at some distance from her own, and Carleton's chair remained empty at Madeleine's side.

At first this was uncomfortably evident, but Madeleine was in gay spirits, and soon the whole party followed her lead, and the conversation was general and in a merry key.

The young hostess had never looked more regally beautiful. Her dark hair, piled high on her head, was adorned with a dainty

12

ornament which, though only a twisted ribbon, was shaped like a crown, and gave her the effect of an imperious queen. Her low-cut gown of pale yellow satin was severe of line and accented her stately bearing, while her exquisitely modelled neck and shoulders were as white and pure as those of a marble statue. Save for a double row of pearls around her throat, she wore no ornaments, but on the morrow Carleton's gift of magnificent diamonds would grace her bridal costume. The combination of haughty imperial beauty and a dazzling witchery of mood was irresistible, and the men and girls alike realized that never before had Madeleine seemed so wonderful.

After the dessert was placed on the table, Willard could stand it no longer, and, leaving his own place, he calmly appropriated Carleton's vacant chair.

Madeleine did not reprove him, and Kitty French took occasion to whisper to her neighbor:

"'Twere better by far to have matched our fair cousin to brave Lochinvar.'"

Mrs. Markham overheard the quotation, and a look of pain came into her eyes. But it was all too late now, and to-morrow Madeleine would be irrevocably Schuyler Carleton's wife.

After dinner coffee was served in the cozy library. Madeleine preferred this room to the more elaborately furnished drawing-room, and to-night her word was law.

But suddenly her mood changed. For no apparent reason her gay spirits vanished, her smile faded away, and a pathetic droop curved the corners of her beautiful mouth.

At about ten o'clock she said abruptly, though gently, "I wish you'd all go to bed. Unless you girls get some beauty sleep, you won't look pretty at my wedding to-morrow."

"I'm quite ready to go," declared Kitty French with some tact, for she saw that Madeleine was nervous and strung up to a high tension.

"I, too," exclaimed Molly Gardner, and the two girls said good-night and went upstairs.

Two or three young men who had been dinner guests also made their adieux, and Tom Willard said, "Well, I may as well toddle to my comforts of home, as understood by a country innkeeper."

Madeleine said good-night to him kindly enough, but without jest or gaiety. Tom looked at her curiously for a moment, and then, gently kissing her hand, he went away.

Mrs. Markham, having seen Miss Morton comfortably installed in what had been Tom's room, returned to the library to offer her services to Madeleine.

13

But the girl only thanked her, saying, "There is nothing you can do to-night. I want to be alone for an hour or two. I will stay here in the library for a time, and I'd like to have you send Cicely to me."

A few moments later Cicely Dupuy came in, bringing some letters and papers. She was Miss Van Norman's private secretary, and admirably did she fill the post. Quick-witted, clever, deft of hand and brain, she answered notes, kept accounts, and in many ways made herself invaluable to her employer.

Moreover, Madeleine liked her. Cicely was of a charming personality. Small, fair, with big, childish blue eyes and a rose-leaf skin, she was a pretty picture to look at.

"Sit down," said Madeleine, "and make a little list of some final matters I want you to attend to to-morrow."

Cicely sat down, and, taking pencil and tablet from the library table, made the lists as Madeleine directed. This occupied but a short time, and then Miss Van Norman said wearily:

"You may go now, Cicely. Go to bed at once, dear. You will have much to do to-morrow. And please tell Marie I shall not need her services to-night. She may go to her room. I shall sit here for an hour or more, and I will answer these notes. I wish to be alone."

"Very well, Miss Van Norman," said Cicely, and, taking the lists she had made, she went softly from the room.

14

III

A CRY IN THE NIGHT

"Help!"

The loud cry of a single word was not repeated, but repetition was unnecessary, for the sound rang through the old Van Norman house, and carried its message of fear and horror to all, awake or sleeping, within its walls.

It was about half-past eleven that same night, and Cicely Dupuy, still fully dressed, flew from her bedroom out into the hall.

Seeing a light downstairs, and hearing the servants' bells, one after another, as if rung by a frantic hand, she hesitated a moment only, and then ran downstairs.

In the lower hall Schuyler Carleton, with a dazed expression on his white, drawn face, was uncertainly pushing various electric buttons which, in turn, flashed lights on or off, or rang bells in distant parts of the house.

For a moment Cicely stared straight at the man. Their eyes met, their gaze seemed to concentrate, and they stood motionless, as if spellbound.

This crisis was broken in upon by Marie, Madeleine's French maid, who came running downstairs in a hastily donned negligée.

"Mon Dieu!" she cried. "Ou est Mademoiselle?"

With a start, Carleton turned from Cicely, and still with that dazed look on his face, he motioned Marie toward the wide doorway of the library. The girl took a step toward the threshold, and then, with a shriek, paused, and ventured no further.

Cicely, as if impelled by an unseen force, slowly turned and followed Marie's movements, and as the girl screamed, Cicely grasped her tightly by the arm, and the two stood staring in at the library door.

What they saw was Madeleine Van Norman, seated in a chair at the library table. Her right arm was on the table, and her head, which had fallen to one side, was supported by her right shoulder. Her eyes were partly closed, and her lips were parted, and the position of the rigid figure left no need for further evidence that this was not a natural sleep.

But further evidence there was. Miss Van Norman still wore her yellow satin gown, but the beautiful embroidered bodice was stained a dull red, and a crimson stream was even then spreading its way down the shimmering breadths of the trailing skirt.

15

On the table, near the outstretched white hand, lay a Venetian dagger. This dagger was well known to the onlookers. It had lain on the library table for many years, and though ostensibly for the purpose of a paper-cutter, it was rarely used as such. Its edges were too sharp to cut paper satisfactorily, and, moreover, it was a wicked-looking affair, and many people had shuddered as they touched it. It had a history, too, and Richard Van Norman used to tell his guests of dark deeds in which the dagger had taken part while it was still in Italy.

Madeleine herself had had a horror of the weapon, though she had often admitted the fascination of its marvellous workmanship, and had said upon several occasions that the thing fairly hypnotized her, and some day she should kill herself or somebody else with it.

From an instinctive sense of duty, Marie started forward, as if to help her mistress, then with a convulsive shudder she screamed again and clasped her hands before her eyes to shut out the awful sight.

Cicely, too, moved slowly toward the silent figure, then turned and again gazed steadfastly at Schuyler Carleton.

There must have been interrogation in her eyes, for the man pointed toward the table, and Cicely looked again, to notice there a bit of paper with writing on it.

She made no motion toward it, but the expression on her face changed to one of bewildered surprise. Before she had time to speak, however, the other people of the house all at once began to gather in the hall.

Mrs. Markham came first, and though when she saw Madeleine she turned very white and seemed about to faint, she bravely went at once toward the girl, and gently tried to raise the fallen head.

She felt a firm grasp on her shoulder, and turned to see Miss Morton, with a stern, set face, at her side.

"Don't touch her," said Miss Morton, in a whisper. "Telephone for a doctor quickly."

"But she's dead," declared Mrs. Markham, at the same time bursting into violent sobs.

"We do not know; we hope not," went on Miss Morton, and without another word she led Mrs. Markham to a sofa, and sat her down rather suddenly, and then went herself straight to the telephone.

As she reached it she paused only to inquire the name of the family physician.

Harris, the butler, with difficulty articulated the name of Doctor Hills and his telephone number, and without further inquiry Miss Morton called for him.

16

"Is this Doctor Hills?" she said when her call was answered. "Yes; this is the Van Norman house. Come here at once. . . . No matter; you must come at once—it is very important—a matter of life and death. . . . I am Miss Morton. I am in charge here. Yes, come immediately! Good-by."

Miss Morton hung up the receiver and turned to the frightened group of servants.

"You can do nothing," she said, "and you may as well return to your rooms. Harris may stay, and one of the parlor maids."

Miss Morton had an imperious air, and instinctively the servants obeyed her.

But Cicely Dupuy was not so ready to accept the dictum of a stranger. She stepped forward and, facing Miss Morton, said quietly, "Mrs. Markham is housekeeper, as well as Miss Van Norman's chaperon. The servants are accustomed to take their orders from her."

Miss Morton returned Cicely's direct gaze. "You see Mrs. Markham," she said, pointing to the sofa, where that lady had entirely collapsed, and, with her head in a pillow, was shaking with convulsive sobs. "She is for the moment quite incapable of giving orders. As the oldest person present, and as a life-long friend of Mr. Richard Van Norman, I shall take the liberty of directing affairs in the present crisis." Then, in a softer tone and with a glance toward Madeleine, Miss Morton continued, "I trust in view of the awfulness of the occasion you will give me your sympathy and co-operation, that we may work in harmony."

Cicely gave Miss Morton a curious glance that might have meant almost anything, but with a slight inclination of her head she said only, "Yes, madam."

Then Kitty French and Molly Gardner came downstairs and stood trembling on the threshold.

"What is it?" whispered Kitty. "What's the matter with Madeleine?"

"Something dreadful has happened," said Miss Morton, meeting them at the door. "I have telephoned for Doctor Hills and he will be here soon. Until then we can do nothing."

"But we can try to help Maddy," exclaimed Kitty, starting toward the still figure by the table. "Oh, is she hurt? I thought she had fainted!"

As the two girls saw the dread sight, Miss Gardner fainted herself, and Miss Morton bade Marie, who stood shivering in the hall, take care of her.

Relieved at having something to do, Marie shook the girl and

17

dashed water in her face until she regained consciousness, the others, meanwhile, paying little attention.

Schuyler Carleton stood leaning against the doorpost, his eyes fixed on Madeleine's tragic figure, while Kitty French, who had dropped into a chair, sat with her hands tightly clasped, also gazing at the sad picture.

Although it seemed hours to those who awaited him, it was but a few moments before the doctor came.

Doctor Hills was a clean-cut, alert-looking young man, and his quick eyes seemed to take in every detail of the scene at a glance.

He went straight to the girl at the table and bent over her. Only the briefest examination was necessary before he said gently, "She is quite dead. She has been stabbed with this dagger. It entered a large blood vessel just over her heart, and she bled to death. Who killed her?"

Even as he spoke his eye fell on the written paper which lay on the table. With one of his habitually quick gestures he snatched it up and read it to himself, while a look of great surprise dawned on his face. Immediately he read it aloud:

I am wholly miserable, and unless the clouds lift I must end my life. I love S., but he does not love me.

After he finished reading, Doctor Hills stood staring at the paper, and looked utterly perplexed.

"I should have said it was not a suicide," he declared, "but this message seems to indicate that it is. Is this written in Miss Van Norman's hand?"

Miss Morton, who stood at the doctor's side, took the paper and scrutinized it.

"It is," she said. "Yes, certainly that is Miss Van Norman's writing. I had a letter from her only a few days ago, and I recognize it perfectly."

"Let me see it," said Mrs. Markham, in a determined, though rather timid way. "I am more familiar with Madeleine's writing than a stranger can possibly be."

Miss Morton handed the paper to the housekeeper without a word, while the doctor, waiting, wondered why these two women seemed so out of sympathy with each other.

"Yes, it is surely Madeleine's writing," agreed Mrs. Markham, her glasses dropping off as her eyes filled with tears.

"Then I suppose she killed herself, poor girl," said the doctor. "She must have been desperate, indeed, for it was a strong blow that drove the steel in so deeply. Who first discovered her here?"

18

"I did," said Schuyler Carleton, stepping forward. His face was almost as white as the dead girl's, and he was scarcely able to make his voice heard. "I came in with a latch-key, and found her here, just as you see her now."

As Carleton spoke Cicely Dupuy stared at him with that curious expression that seemed to show something more than grief and horror. Her emotional bewilderment was not surprising in view of the awful situation, but her look was a strange one, and for some reason it greatly disconcerted the man.

None of this escaped the notice of Doctor Hills. Looking straight at Carleton, but with a kindly expression replacing the stern look on his face, he went on:

"And when you came in, was Miss Van Norman just as we see her now?"

"Practically," said Carleton. "I couldn't believe her dead. And I tried to rouse her. Then I saw the dagger on the floor at her feet——"

"On the floor?" interrupted Doctor Hills.

"Yes," replied Carleton, whose agitation was increasing, and who had sunk into a chair because of sheer inability to stand. "It was on the floor at her feet—right at her feet. I picked it up, and there was blood on it—there is blood on it—and I laid it on the table. And then I saw the paper—the paper that says she killed herself. And then—and then I turned on the lights and rang the servants' bells, and Cicely—Miss Dupuy—came, and the others, and—that's all."

Schuyler Carleton had with difficulty concluded his narration, and he sat clenching his hands and biting his lips as if at the very limit of his powers of endurance.

Doctor Hills again glanced round the assembly in that quick way of his, and said:

"Did any of you have reason to think Miss Van Norman had any thought of taking her own life?"

For a moment no one spoke, and then Kitty French, who, in a despairing, miserable way, was huddled in the depths of a great arm-chair, said:

"I have heard Madeleine say that some time she would kill herself with that horrid old dagger. I wish I had stolen it and buried it long ago!"

Doctor Hills turned to Mrs. Markham. "Did you have any reason to fear this?" he inquired.

"No," she replied; "and I do not think Madeleine meant she would voluntarily use that dagger. She only meant she had a superstitious dread of the thing."

19

"Do you understand her reference to her own unhappiness in this bit of writing?" went on the doctor.

"Yes, I think I do," said Mrs. Markham in a low voice.

"That is enough for the present," said the doctor, as if to interrupt further confidences. "Although it is difficult to believe a stab of that nature could be self-inflicted, it is possible, and this communication seems to leave no room for doubt. Now, the law of New Jersey requires that in case of a death not by natural means the county physician shall be summoned, and further proceedings are entirely at his discretion. I shall therefore be obliged to send for Doctor Leonard before disturbing the body in any way. He will probably not arrive in less than an hour or so, and I would advise that you ladies retire. You can of course do nothing to help, and as I shall remain in charge, you may as well get what rest you can during the night."

"I thank you for your consideration, Doctor Hills," said Mrs. Markham, who seemed to have recovered her calmness, "but I prefer to stay here. I could not rest after this awful shock, and I cannot stay away from Madeleine."

Kitty French and Molly Gardner, who, clasped in each other's arms, were shivering with excitement and grief, begged to be allowed to stay, too, but Doctor Hills peremptorily ordered them to go to their rooms. Cicely Dupuy was allowed to stay, as in her position of social secretary she might know much of Madeleine's private affairs. For the same reason Marie was detained, while Doctor Hills asked her a few questions.

Schuyler Carleton sat rigidly in his chair, as immovable as a statue. This man puzzled Doctor Hills. And yet it was surely shock enough almost to unhinge a man's brain thus to find his intended bride the night before his wedding.

But Carleton seemed absorbed in emotions other than those of grief. Though his face was impassive, his eyes darted about the room looking at one after another of the shocked and terrified group, returning always to the still figure at the table, and as quickly turning his gaze away, as if the sight were unbearable, as indeed it was.

He seemed like a man stunned with the awfulness of the tragedy, and yet conscious of a care, a responsibility, which he could not shake off.

If, inadvertently, his eyes met those of Miss Dupuy, he shifted his gaze immediately. If by chance he encountered Mrs. Markham's sad glance, he turned away, unable to bear it. In a word, he was like a man at the limit of his endurance, and seemed veritably on the verge of collapse.

IV

SUICIDE OR —?

Miss Morton, also, seemed to have distracting thoughts. She sat down on the sofa beside Mrs. Markham, then she jumped up suddenly and started for the door, only to turn about and resume her seat on the sofa. Here she sat for a few moments apparently in deep thought. Then she rose, and slowly stalked from the room and went upstairs.

After a few moments, Marie, the French maid, also rose and silently left the room.

Having concluded it was a case for the county physician, Doctor Hills apparently considered that his personal responsibility was at an end, and he sat quietly awaiting the coming of his colleague.

After a time, Miss Morton returned, and again took her seat on the sofa. She looked excited and a little flurried, but strove to appear calm.

It was a dreadful hour. Only rarely any one spoke, and though glances sometimes shot from the eyes of one to the eyes of another, each felt his gaze oftenest impelled toward that dread, beautiful figure by the table.

At last Schuyler Carleton, with an evident effort, said suddenly, "Oughtn't we to send for Tom Willard?"

Mrs. Markham gave a start. "Of course we must," she said. "Poor Tom! He must be told. Who will tell him?"

"I will," volunteered Miss Morton, and Doctor Hills looked up, amazed at her calm tone. This woman puzzled him, and he could not understand her continued attempts at authority in a household where she was a comparative stranger. And yet might it not be merely a kind consideration for those who were nearer and dearer to the principals of this awful tragedy?

But even as he thought this over, Miss Morton had gone to the telephone, her heavy silk gown rustling as she crossed the room, and her every movement assertive of her own importance.

Calling up the Mapleton Inn, she succeeded, after several attempts, in rousing some of its occupants, and finally was in communication with young Willard himself. She did not tell him of the tragedy, but only asked him to come over to the house at once, as something serious had happened, and returned to her seat with a murmured observation that Tom would arrive as soon as possible.

Again the little group lapsed into silence. Cicely Dupuy was very

21

nervous, and kept picking at her handkerchief, quite unconscious that she was ruining its delicate lace edge.

Doctor Hills glanced furtively from one to another. Many things puzzled him, but most of all he was at a loss to understand the suicide of this beautiful girl on the very eve of her wedding.

At last Tom Willard came.

Miss Morton met him at the door, and took him into the drawing-room before he could turn toward the library.

Schuyler Carleton's frantic touches on various electric buttons had turned on all the lights in the drawing-room. As no one had noticed this, the great apartment had remained illuminated as if for a festivity, and the soft, bright lights fell on the floral bower and the elaborate decorations that had been arranged for the wedding day.

"What is it?" asked Tom, his own face white with an impending sense of dread as he looked into Miss Morton's eyes.

As gently as possible, but in her own straightforward and inevitably somewhat abrupt way, Miss Morton told him.

"I want to warn you," she said, "to prepare for a shock, and I think it kinder to tell you the truth at once. Your cousin Madeleine—Miss Van Norman—has taken her own life."

"What?" Tom almost shouted the word, and his face showed an absolutely uncomprehending amazement.

"She killed herself to-night," Miss Morton went on, whose efforts were now directed toward making the young man understand, rather than towards sparing his feelings.

But Tom could not seem to grasp it. "What do you mean?" he said, catching her by both arms. "Madeleine? Killed herself?"

"Yes," said Miss Morton, shaken out of her own calm by Tom's excited voice. "In the library, after we had all gone to bed, she stabbed herself with that horrible paper-cutter thing. Did you know she was unhappy?"

"Unhappy? No; why should she be? To-morrow was to have been her wedding day!"

"To-day," corrected Miss Morton. "It is already the day on which our dear Madeleine was to have become a bride. And instead——" Glancing around the brilliant room and at the bridal bower, Miss Morton's composure gave way entirely, and she sobbed hysterically. At this Cicely Dupuy came across from the library. Putting her arm around Miss Morton, she led the sobbing woman away, and without a word to Tom Willard gave him a glance which seemed to say that he must look out for himself, for her duty was to attend Miss Morton.

As the two women left the drawing-room Tom followed them. He walked slowly, and stared about as if uncertain where to go. He

22

paused a moment midway in the room, and, stooping, picked up some small object from the carpet, which he put in his waistcoat pocket.

A moment more and he had crossed the hall and stood at the library door, gazing at the scene which had already shocked and saddened the others.

With a groan, as of utter anguish, Tom involuntarily put up one hand before his eyes.

Then, pulling himself together with an effort, he seemed to dash away a tear, and walked into the room, saying almost harshly, "What does it mean?"

Doctor Hills rose to meet him, and by way of a brief explanation he put into Tom's hand the paper he had found on the table. Tom read the written message, and looked more stupefied than ever. With a sudden gesture he turned towards Schuyler Carleton and said in a low voice, "but you did love her, didn't you?"

"I did," replied Carleton simply.

"Why should she have thought you didn't?" went on Tom, looking at the paper, and seeming to soliloquize rather than to address his question to any one else.

As this was the first time that the "S." in Madeleine's note had been openly assumed to stand for Schuyler Carleton, there was a stir of excitement all round the room.

"I don't know," said Carleton, but a dull, red flush spread over his white face and his voice trembled.

"You don't know!" said Tom, in cutting tones. "Man, you must know."

But no reply was made, and, dropping into a chair, Tom buried his face in both hands and remained thus for a long time.

Tom Willard was a large, stout man, and possessed of the genial and merry demeanor which so often accompanies avoirdupois. Save for his occasional, though really rare, bursts of temper, Tom was always in joking and laughing mood.

To see him thus in an agonized, speechless despair deeply affected Mrs. Markham. Tom had always been a favorite with her, and not even Madeleine had regretted more than she the estrangement between Richard Van Norman and his nephew. And even as Mrs. Markham looked at the bowed head of the great strong man she suddenly bethought herself for the first time that Tom was now heir to the Van Norman fortune.

She wondered if he had himself yet realized it; and then she scolded herself for letting such thoughts intrude so unfittingly soon. And yet she well knew that it would not be in ordinary human nature long to ignore the fact of such a sudden change of fortunes.

23

As she looked at Tom her glance strayed toward Mr. Carleton, and then the thought struck her that what Tom had gained this man had lost. For had Madeleine lived the Van Norman money would have been, in a way, at the disposal of her husband. The girl's death then would make Tom a rich man, while Schuyler Carleton would remain poor. He had always been poor, or at least far from wealthy, and more than one gossip was of the opinion that he had wooed Miss Van Norman not entirely because of disinterested love for her.

While Mrs. Markham was busy with these fast-following thoughts a voice in the doorway made her look up.

A quiet, unimportant-looking man stood there, and was respectfully addressing Doctor Hills.

"I'm Hunt, sir," he said, "a plain-clothes man from headquarters."

The three men in the room gave a start of surprise, and each turned an inquiring look at the newcomer.

"Who sent you? And what for?" asked Doctor Hills.

"I've been here all night, sir. I'm on guard in the present room upstairs."

"I engaged him," said Mrs. Markham. "Madeleine's presents are very valuable, and although the jewels are still in the bank, the silver and other things upstairs are worth a large amount, and I thought best to have this man remain here during the night."

"A very wise precaution, Mrs. Markham," said Doctor Hills; "and why did you leave your post, my man?"

"The butler told me of what had happened, and I wondered if I might be of any service down here. I left the butler in charge of the room while I came down to inquire."

"Very thoughtful of you," said Doctor Hills, with a nod of appreciation; "and while I hardly think so, we may have use for you before the night is over. I am expecting Doctor Leonard, the county physician, and until he comes I can do nothing. I am sure the room above is sufficiently guarded for the time being, so suppose you sit down here a few minutes and wait."

Mr. Hunt chose to take a seat in the hall, just outside the library door, and thus added one more solemn presence to the quietly waiting group.

And now Doctor Hills had occasion to add another puzzling condition to those that had already confronted him.

Almost every one in the room was curiously affected by the appearance of this detective, or plain-clothes man, as he was called.

Schuyler Carleton gave a start, and his pale face became whiter yet.

Cicely Dupuy looked at him, and then turning her glance

24

toward Mr. Hunt, whom she could see through the doorway, she favored the latter with a stare of such venomous hatred that Doctor Hills with difficulty repressed an exclamation.

Cicely's big blue eyes roved from Hunt to Carleton and back again, and her little hands clenched as with a firm resolve of some sort in her mind; she seemed to brace herself for action.

Her hovering glances annoyed Carleton; he grew nervous and at last stared straight at her, when her own eyes dropped, and she blushed rosy red.

But this side-play was observed by no one but Doctor Hills, for the others were evidently absorbed in serious thoughts of their own concerning the advent of Mr. Hunt.

Tom Willard stared at him in a sort of perplexity; but Tom's good-natured face had worn that perplexed look ever since he had heard the awful news. He seemed unable to understand, or even to grasp the facts so clearly visible before him.

But Miss Morton was more disturbed than any one else. She looked at Hunt, and an expression of fear came into her eyes. She fidgeted about, she felt in her pocket, she changed her seat twice, and she repeatedly asked Doctor Hills if he thought Doctor Leonard would arrive soon.

Doctor Leonard did not live in Mapleton, but motored over from his home in a nearby village. He was a stranger to all those awaiting him in the Van Norman house, with the exception of Doctor Hills. Unlike that pleasant-mannered young man, Doctor Leonard was middle aged, of a crusty disposition and curt speech.

When he came, Doctor Hills presented him to the ladies, and before he had time to introduce the two men, Doctor Leonard said crossly, "Put the women out. I cannot conduct this affair with petticoats and hysterics around me."

Though not meant to reach the ears of the ladies, the speech was fairly audible, and with a trace of indignation Miss Morton arose and left the room. Mrs. Markham followed her, and Cicely went also.

Doctor Leonard closed the library doors, and, turning to Doctor Hills, asked for a concise statement of what had happened.

In his straightforward manner Doctor Hills gave him a brief outline of the case, including all the necessary details.

"And yet," he concluded, "even in the face of that written message, I cannot think it a suicide."

"Of course it's a suicide," declared Doctor Leonard in his blustering way; "there is no question whatever. That written confession which you all declare to be in her handwriting is ample proof that the girl killed herself. Of course you had to send for me—

25

the stupid old laws of New Jersey make it imperative that I shall be dragged out many miles away from my home for every death that isn't in conventional death-bed fashion; but there is no suspicion of foul play here. The poor girl chose to kill herself, and she has done so with the means which she found near at hand. I will write the burial certificate and leave it with you. There is no occasion for the coroner."

"Thank God for that!" exclaimed Schuyler Carleton, in a fervent tone.

"Amen," said Tom. "It's dreadful enough to think of poor Maddy as she is, but had it been any one else who——"

Unheeding the ejaculations of the two men, Doctor Hills said earnestly, "But, Doctor, if it had not been for the written paper, would you have called it suicide?"

"That has nothing to do with the case," declared Doctor Leonard testily. "The paper is there, and is authentic. No sane man could doubt that it is a suicide after that."

"But, Doctor Leonard, it would seem impossible for a woman to stab herself at that angle, and with such an astonishing degree of force; also to pull the dagger from the wound, cast it on the floor, and then to place her arm in that particular position on the table."

"Why do you say in that particular position?"

"Because the position of her right arm is as if thrown there carelessly, and not as if flung there in a death agony."

"You are imaginative, Doctor Hills. The facts may not seem possible, but since they are the facts you must admit that they are possible."

"Very well, Doctor Leonard, I accept your decision, and I relinquish all professional responsibility in the matter."

"You may do so. There is no occasion for mystery or question. It is a sad affair, indeed, but no crime is indicated beyond that of self-destruction. The written confession hints at the motive for the deed, but that is outside my jurisdiction. Who is the man in the hall? I fancied him a detective."

"He is; that is, he is a man from headquarters who is here to watch over the bridal gifts. He came down-stairs thinking we might require his services in another way."

"Send him back to his post. There is no work for detectives, just because a young girl chose to end her unhappy life."

Doctor Hills opened the library door and directed Hunt to return to his place in the present room.

Doctor Leonard, still with his harsh and disagreeable manner, advised Willard and Carleton to go to their homes, saying he and

26

Doctor Hills would remain in charge of the library for the rest of the night.

Doctor Hills found the women in the drawing-room, awaiting such message as Doctor Leonard might have for them. Doctor Hills told them all that Doctor Leonard had said, and advised them to retire, as the next day would be indeed a difficult and sorrowful one.

V

A CASE FOR THE CORONER

It was characteristic of Miss Morton that she went straight to her own room and shut the door. Mrs. Markham, on the other hand, went to the room occupied by Kitty French. Molly Gardner was there, too, and the two girls, robed in kimonas, were sitting, white-faced and tearful-eyed, waiting for some further news from the room whence they had been banished.

Mrs. Markham told them what Doctor Leonard had said, but Kitty French broke out impetuously, "Madeleine never killed herself, never! I know she always said that about the dagger, but she never really meant it, and any way she never would have done it the night before her wedding. I tell you she didn't do it! It was some horrid burglar who came in to steal her presents, who killed her."

"I would almost rather it had been so, Kitty dear," said Mrs. Markham, gently stroking the brow of the excited girl; "but it could not have been, for we have very strong locks and bolts against burglars, and Harris is very careful in his precautions for our safety."

"I don't care! Maddy never killed herself. She wouldn't do it, I know her too well. Oh, dear! now there won't be any wedding at all! Isn't it dreadful to think of that decorated room, and the bower we planned for the bride!"

At these thoughts Kitty's tears began to flow afresh, and Molly, who was already limp from weeping, joined her.

"There, there," said Mrs. Markham, gently patting Molly's shoulder. "Don't cry so, dearie. It can't do any good, and you'll just make yourself ill."

"But I don't understand," said Molly, as she mopped her eyes with her wet ball of a handkerchief; "why did she kill herself?"

"I don't know," said Mrs. Markham, but her expression seemed to betoken a sad suspicion.

"She didn't kill herself," reiterated Kitty. "I stick to that, but if she did, I know why."

This feminine absence of logic was unremarked by her hearers, who both said, "Why?"

"Because Schuyler didn't love her enough," said Kitty earnestly. "She just worshipped him, and he used to care more for her, but lately he hasn't."

"How do you know?" asked Molly.

28

"Oh, Madeleine didn't tell me," returned Kitty. "I just gathered it. I've been here 'most a week—you know I came several days before you did, Molly—and I've noticed her a lot. Oh, I don't mean I spied on her, or anything horrid. Only, I couldn't help seeing that she wished Mr. Carleton would be more attentive."

"Why, I thought he was awfully attentive," said Molly.

"Oh, attentive, yes. I don't exactly mean that. But there was something lacking,—don't you think so, Mrs. Markham?"

"Yes, Kitty, I do think so. In fact, I know that Mr. Carleton didn't give Madeleine the heart-whole affection that she gave him. But I hoped it would all turn out right, and I surely never dreamed it was such a serious matter as to bring Madeleine to this. But she was a reserved, proud nature, and if she thought Mr. Carleton had ceased to love her, I know she would far rather die than marry him."

"But she could have refused to marry him," cried Molly. "She didn't have to kill herself to get rid of him."

"She didn't kill herself," stubbornly repeated Kitty, but Mrs. Markham said:

"You don't understand Maddy's nature, Molly; she must have had some sudden and positive proof of Mr. Carleton's lack of true affection for her to drive her to this step. But once convinced that he did not care for her, I know her absolute despair would impel her to the desperate deed."

"Why didn't he love her?" said Molly, who could see no reason why any man shouldn't love the magnificent Madeleine.

"I think," said Kitty slowly, "there was somebody else."

"How did you know that?" exclaimed Mrs. Markham sharply, as if she had detected Kitty in some wrongdoing.

"I don't know it, but I can't help thinking so. Madeleine has sometimes asked me if I didn't think most men preferred gentle, timid dispositions to a strong, capable nature like her own. Of course she didn't express it just like that, but she hinted at it so wistfully, that I told her no, she was the splendidest, most adorable woman in the whole world. I meant it, too, but at the same time I do think men 'most always love the soft, tractable kind of girls, that are not so imperious and awe-inspiring as Maddy was."

Surely Kitty ought to know, for she was the most delicious type of soft, tractable femininity.

Her round, dimpled face was positively peachy, and her curling tendrils of goldy hair clustered round a low white brow, above appealing violet eyes. A man might admire the haughty Madeleine, but he would caressingly love bewitching little Kitty, and would involuntarily feel a sense of protection toward her, because of the shy trustfulness in her glance.

This was not entirely ingenuous, for wise little Kitty quite understood her own charm, but it was natural, and in no way forced; and she was quite content that her lines had fallen in her own pleasant places, and she left the magnificent Madeleines of the world to pursue their own rôles. But she had admired and loved Maddy Van Norman, and just because of their differing natures, had understood why Schuyler Carleton's affection was tempered with a certain sense of inferiority.

"You know," she went on, as if thinking aloud, "everybody was a little afraid of magnificent Maddy. She was so superb, so regal. You couldn't imagine yourself cuddling her!"

"I should say not!" exclaimed Molly. "I could only imagine salaaming to her, or deferentially kissing her hand."

"Yes, that's what I mean. Well, Mr. Carleton got tired of that stilted kind of an attitude,—or, at least, she thought he did. I don't know, I'm sure, but she was possessed with a notion that he cared for some other girl,—some one of the clinging rosebud sort."

"Do you know this?" asked Mrs. Markham; "I mean, do you know that Maddy thought this?"

"Yes, I know it," asserted Kitty, with a wag of her wise little head. "I tried to persuade her that no clinging rosebud could rival a tall, proud lily, but she thoroughly believed there was some one else."

"But Mr. Carleton was to marry her," said Mrs. Markham. "I can't believe he would do that if he loved another."

"That's what bothered Maddy," said Kitty; "she knew how honorable Mr. Carleton had always been, and she said that as he was engaged to her, he would think it his duty to marry her, even though his heart belonged to some one else."

"Oh, pshaw!" said Molly. "If he was going to marry her, and didn't love her, it was because of her fortune. Probably his rosebud girl hasn't a cent."

"Don't talk like that," said Kitty, shuddering. "Somehow it seems disloyal to both of them."

"But it is all true," said Mrs. Markham sadly. "Madeleine has never been of a confidential nature, but I know that she had the idea Kitty tells of, and I fear it was true. And I may be disloyal, or even unjust, but I can't help thinking Schuyler was attracted by Maddy's money. He is proud and ambitious, and he would be quite in his element as the head of a fine establishment, with plenty of money to spend on it."

"Well, he'll never have it now," said Molly, and as this brought back the realization of the awful event that had happened, both girls burst into crying again.

30

Mrs. Markham, herself with overwrought nerves, found she could do nothing to comfort the girls, so left them and went to commune with her grief in her own room.

Meantime the two doctors alone in the library were still in discussion.

"Well, what do you want?" inquired Doctor Leonard angrily. "Do you want to imply, and with no evidence whatever, that the girl died by some hand other than her own? Do you want to involve the family in the expense and unpleasant publicity of a coroner's inquest, when there is not only no reason for such a proceeding, but there is every reason against it?"

"I want nothing but to get at the truth," rejoined Doctor Hills, a little ruffled himself. "I hold that a young woman, unless endowed with unusual strength, or possibly under stress of intense passion, could not inflict upon herself a blow strong enough to drive that dagger to the hilt in her own breast, pull it forth again, and cast it on the floor, and after that place her arm in the position it now occupies."

Doctor Leonard looked thoughtful. "I agree with you," he said slowly; "that is, I agree that it does not seem as if a woman could do that. But, my dear Doctor Hills, Miss Van Norman did do that. We know she did, from her own written confession, and also by the theory of elimination. What else could have happened? Have you any suggestion to advance?"

Doctor Hills was somewhat taken aback at Doctor Leonard's suddenness. Up to this moment the county physician had stoutly maintained that the case was a suicide beyond any question, and then, turning, he had put the question to the younger doctor in such a way that Doctor Hills was not quite ready with an answer.

"No," he said hesitatingly; "I have no theory to advance, and, moreover, I do not consider this an occasion for theories. But we must ascertain the facts. I state it as a fact that a woman could not stab herself as Miss Van Norman is stabbed, withdraw the dagger, and then place her right arm on the table in the position you see it."

"And I assert that you are stating what is not a fact, but merely your own opinion."

Doctor Hills looked disconcerted at this. His companion was an older and far more experienced man than himself, and not only did Doctor Hills have no desire to antagonize him, but he wished to show him the deference that was justly his due.

"You are right," he said frankly; "it is merely my own opinion. But now will you give me yours, based, not on the written paper, but the position and general effect of the body of Miss Van Norman?"

Put thus on his mettle, Doctor Leonard looked carefully at the dead girl, whose pose was so natural and graceful that she might have been merely sitting there, resting.

He gazed long and intently, and then said, slowly:

"I see your point, Doctor Hills. It was a vigorous blow, suddenly and forcefully given. It could scarcely have been done, had the subject been a frail, slight woman. But Miss Van Norman was of a strong, even athletic build, and her whole physical make-up indicates strength and force of muscle. Your observation as to her apparently natural position is all right so far as it goes; but I have observed more carefully still, and I notice her evident physical strength, which was doubtless greatly aided by her stress of mental passion, and I aver that a woman of her physique could have driven the blow, removed the weapon, and, perhaps even then unconscious, have thrown her arm on the table as we now see it."

"I thank you, Doctor Leonard," said young Hills, "for your patience with me. You are doubtless right, and I frankly admit you have made out a clear case. Miss Van Norman was, indeed, a strong woman. I have been the family physician for several years, and I know her robust constitution. Knowing this, and appreciating your superior judgment as to the possibility of the deed, I am forced to admit your opinion is the true one. And yet——"

"Besides, Doctor Hills," went on Doctor Leonard, as the younger man hesitated, "we cannot, we must not, ignore the written paper. Why should we do so? Those who know, tell us Miss Van Norman wrote it. It is, therefore, her dying statement. Dare we disregard her last message, written in explanation of her otherwise inexplicable act? We may wonder at this suicide, we may shudder at it; but we may not doubt that it is a suicide. That paper is not merely evidence,—it is testimony, it is incontrovertible proof."

Doctor Leonard ceased speaking, and sat silent because he had nothing more to say.

Doctor Hills also sat silent, because, try as he might, he could not feel convinced that the older physician was right. It was absurd, he well knew, but every time he glanced at the relaxed pose of that white right arm on the table, he felt more than ever sure that it had lain there just so when the dagger entered the girl's breast.

As the two men sat there, almost as motionless as the other still figure, both saw the knob of the door turn.

They had closed the double doors leading to the hall, on the arrival of Doctor Leonard, and now the knob of one of them was slowly and noiselessly turning round.

A glance of recognition passed between them, but neither spoke or moved.

32

A moment later, the knob having turned completely round, the door began to open very slowly.

Owing to the position of the two men, it was necessary for the door to be opened far enough to admit the intruder's head before they could be seen, and the doctors waited breathlessly to see who it might be who desired to come stealthily to the library that night.

Doctor Hills, whose thoughts worked quickly, had already assumed it was Mrs. Markham, coming to gaze once more on her beloved mistress; but Doctor Leonard formulated no supposition and merely waited to see.

At the edge of the door appeared first a yellow pompadour, followed by the wide-open blue eyes of Cicely Dupuy. Seeing the two men, she came no further into the room, but gave a sort of gasp, and pulled the door quickly shut again. In the still house, the two listeners could hear her footsteps crossing the hall, and ascending the stairs.

"Curious, that," murmured Doctor Hills. "If she wanted to look once more on Miss Van Norman's face, why so stealthy about it? And if she didn't want that, what did she want?"

"I don't know," rejoined Doctor Leonard; "but I see nothing suspicious about it. Doubtless, she did come for a last glance alone at Miss Van Norman, but, seeing us here, didn't care to enter."

"But she gave a strange little shuddering gasp, as if frightened."

"Natural excitement at the strange and awful conditions now present."

"Yes, no doubt." Doctor Hills spoke a bit impatiently. The phlegmatic attitude of his colleague jarred on his own overwrought nerves, and he rose and walked about the room, now and then stopping to scrutinize anew the victim of the cruel dagger.

At last he stood still, across the table from her, but looking at Doctor Leonard.

"I have no suggestion to make," he said slowly. "I have no theory to offer, but I am firmly convinced that Madeleine Van Norman did not strike the blow that took away her life. Perhaps this is more a feeling or an intuition than a logical conviction, but——" He hesitated and looked intently at the dead girl, as if trying to force the secret from her.

With a sudden start he took a step forward, and as he spoke his voice rang with excitement.

"Doctor Leonard," he said, in a quick, concise voice, "will you look carefully at that dagger?"

"Yes," said the older man, impressed by the other's sudden intensity; and, stepping forward, he scrutinized the dagger as it lay on the table, without, however, touching it.

"There is blood on the handle," went on Doctor Hills.

"Yes, several stains, now dried."

"And do you see any blood on the right hand of Miss Van Norman?"

Startled at the implication, Doctor Leonard bent to examine the cold white hand. Not a trace of blood was on it. Instinctively he looked at the girl's left hand, only to find that also immaculately white.

Doctor Leonard stood upright and pulled himself together.

"I was wrong, Doctor Hills," he said, with a nod which in him betokened an unspoken apology. "It is a case for the coroner."

VI

FESSENDEN COMES

It was about nine o'clock the next morning when Rob Fessenden rang the bell of the Van Norman house. Having heard nothing of the events of the night, he had called to offer any assistance he might give before the ceremony.

The trailing garland of white flowers with fluttering streamers of white ribbon that hung beside the portal struck a chill to his heart.

"What can have happened?" he thought blankly, and confused ideas of motor accidents were thronging his mind as the door was opened for him. The demeanor of the footman at once told him that he was in a house of mourning. Shown into the drawing-room, he was met by Cicely Dupuy.

"Mr. Fessenden!" she exclaimed as she greeted him. "Then you have not heard?"

"I've heard nothing. What is it?"

Poor Miss Dupuy had bravely taken up the burden of telling the sad story to callers who did not know of it, and this was not the first time that morning she had enlightened inquiring friends.

In a few words she told Mr. Fessenden of the events of the night before. He was shocked and sincerely grieved. Although his acquaintance with Miss Van Norman was slight, he was Schuyler Carleton's oldest and best friend, and so he had come from New York the day before in order to take his part at the wedding.

While they were talking Kitty French came in. As Mr. Fessenden began to converse with her Cicely excused herself and left the room.

"Isn't it awful?" began Kitty, and her tear-filled eyes supplemented the trite sentence.

"It is indeed," said Rob Fessenden, taking her hand in spontaneous sympathy. "Why should she do it?"

"She didn't do it," declared Kitty earnestly. "Mr. Fessenden, they all say she killed herself, but I know she didn't. Won't you help me to prove that, and to find out who did kill her?"

"What do you mean, Miss French? Miss Dupuy just told me it was a suicide."

"They all say so, but I know better. Oh, I wish somebody would help me! Molly doesn't think as I do, and I can't do anything all alone."

Miss French's face was small and flower-like, and when she clasped her little hands and bewailed her inability to prove her belief, young Fessenden thought he had never seen such a perfect picture of beautiful helplessness. Without reserve he instantly resolved to aid and advise her to the best of his own ability.

"And Mrs. Markham doesn't think as I do, either," went on Kitty. "Nobody thinks as I do."

"I will think as you do," declared Fessenden, and so potent was the charm of the tearful violet eyes, that he was quite ready to think whatever she dictated. "Only tell me what to think, and what to do about it."

"Why, I think Madeleine didn't kill herself at all. I think somebody else killed her."

"But who would do such a thing? You see, Miss French, I know nothing of the particulars. I saw Miss Van Norman for the first time yesterday."

"Had you never met her before?"

"Oh, yes; a few years ago. But I mean, I came to Mapleton only yesterday, and saw her in the afternoon. I was to be Schuyler's best man, you know, and as he didn't come here to dinner last night, I thought I'd better not come either, though I had been asked. He was a little miffed with Miss Van Norman, you know."

"Yes, I know. Maddy did flirt with Tom, and it always annoyed Mr. Carleton. Did you dine with him?"

"Yes, at his home. I am staying there. By the way, I met Miss Burt there; do you know her?"

"No, not at all. Who is she?"

"She's a companion to Mrs. Carleton, Schuyler's mother. I never saw her until last night at dinner."

"No, I don't know her," repeated Kitty. "I don't believe she was invited to the wedding, for I looked over the list of invitations. Still, her name may have been there. The list was so very long."

"And now there'll be no wedding and no guests."

"No," said Kitty; "only guests at a far different ceremony." Again the deep violet eyes filled with tears, and Fessenden was conscious of a longing to comfort and help the poor little girl thrown thus suddenly into the first tragedy of her life.

"It would be dreadful enough if she had died from an illness," he said; "but this added awfulness——"

"Yes," interrupted Kitty; "but to me the worst part is for them to say she killed herself,—and I know she didn't. Why, Maddy was too fine and big-natured to do such a cowardly thing."

"She seemed so to me, too, though of course I didn't know her so well as you did."

36

"No, I'm one of her nearest friends,—though Madeleine was never one to have really intimate friends. But as her friend, I want to try to do what I can to put her right in the face of the world. And you said you'd help me."

She looked at Fessenden with such hopefully appealing eyes, that he would willingly have helped her in any way he could, but he also realized that it was a very serious proposition this young girl was making.

"I will help you, Miss French," he said gravely. "I know little of the details of the case, but if there is the slightest chance that you may be right, rest assured that you shall be given every chance to prove it."

Kitty French gave a sigh of relief. "Oh, thank you," she said earnestly; "but I'm afraid we cannot do much, however well we intend. Of course I'm merely a guest here, and I have no authority of any sort. And, too, to prove that Maddy did not kill herself would mean having a detective and everything like that."

"I may not be 'everything like that,'" said Fessenden, with a faint smile, "but I am a sort of detective in an amateur way. I've had quite a good deal of experience, and though I wouldn't take a case officially, I'm sure I could at least discover if your suspicions have any grounds."

"But I haven't any suspicions," said Kitty, agitatedly clasping her little hands against her breast; "I've only a feeling, a deep, positive conviction, that Madeleine did not kill herself, and I'm sure I don't know who did kill her."

Fessenden gave that grave smile of his and only said, "That doesn't sound like much to work upon, and yet I would often trust a woman's intuitive knowledge against the most conspicuous clues or evidences."

Kitty thanked him with a smile, but before she could speak, Miss Morton came into the room.

"It's perfectly dreadful," that lady began, in her impetuous way; "they're going to have the coroner after all! Doctor Leonard has sent for him and he may arrive at any minute. Isn't it awful? There'll be an inquest, and the house will be thronged with all sorts of people!"

"Why are they going to have an inquest?" demanded Kitty, whirling around and grasping Miss Morton by her elbows.

"Because," she said, quite as excited as Kitty herself—"because the doctors think that perhaps Madeleine didn't kill herself; that she was—was——"

"Murdered!" exclaimed Kitty. "I knew it! I knew she was! Who killed her?"

37

"Mercy! I don't know," exclaimed Miss Morton, frightened at Kitty's vehemence. "That's what the coroner is coming to find out."

"But who do you think did it? You must have some idea!"

"I haven't! Don't look at me like that! What do you mean?"

"It must have been a burglar," went on Kitty, "because it couldn't have been any one else. But why didn't he steal things? Perhaps he did! We never thought to look!"

"How you do run on! Nobody could steal the presents, because there was a policeman in the house all the time."

"Then, why didn't he catch the burglar?" demanded Kitty, grasping Miss Morton's arm, as if that lady had information that must be dragged from her by force.

Feeling interested in getting at the facts in the case, and thinking that he could learn little from these two excited women, Rob Fessenden turned into the hall just in time to meet Doctor Hills, who was coming from the library.

"May I introduce myself?" he said. "I'm Robert Fessenden, of New York, a lawyer, and I was to have been best man at the wedding. You, I know, are Doctor Hills, and I want to say to you that if the earnest endeavor of an amateur detective would be of any use to you in this matter, it is at your disposal. Mr. Carleton is my old and dear friend, and I need not tell you how he now calls forth my sympathy."

Instinctively, Doctor Hills liked this young man. His frank manner and pleasant, straightforward ways impressed the doctor favorably, and he shook hands warmly as he said, "This is most kind of you, Mr. Fessenden, and you may prove the very man we need. At first, we were all convinced that Miss Van Norman's death was a suicide; and though the evidence still strongly points to that, I am sure that there is a possibility, at least, that it is not true."

"May I learn the details of the case? May I go into the library?" said Fessenden, hesitating to approach the closed door until invited.

"Yes, indeed; I'll take you in at once. Doctor Leonard, who is in there, is the county physician, and, though a bit brusque in his manner, he is an honest old soul, and does unflinchingly what he judges to be his duty."

Neither then nor at any time, neither to Doctor Leonard himself nor to any one else, did Doctor Hills ever mention the difference of opinion which the two men had held for so long the night before, nor did he tell how he had proved his own theory so positively that Doctor Leonard had been obliged to confess himself wrong. It was not in Doctor Hills' nature to say "I told you so," and, fully appreciating this, Doctor Leonard said nothing either, but threw

38

himself into the case heart and soul in his endeavors to seek truth and justice.

Fessenden and Doctor Hills entered the library, where everything was much as it had been the night before. At one time the doctors had been about to move the body to a couch, and to remove the disfigured gown, but after Doctor Leonard had been persuaded to agree with Doctor Hills' view of the case, they had left everything untouched until the coroner should come.

The discovery of this was a satisfaction to Robert Fessenden. His detective instinct had begun to assert itself, and he was glad of an opportunity to examine the room before the arrival of the coroner. Though not seeming unduly curious, his eyes darted about in an eager search for possible clues of any sort. Without touching them, he examined the dagger, the written paper, the appointments of the library table, and the body itself, with its sweet, sad face, its drooping posture, and its tragically stained raiment.

In true detective fashion he scrutinized the carpet, glanced at the window fastenings, and noted the appointments of the library table.

The only thing Fessenden touched, however, was a lead pencil which lay on the pen-rack. It was an ordinary pencil, but he gazed intently at the gilt lettering stamped upon it, and then returned it to its place.

Again he glanced quickly but carefully at every article on the table, and then, taking a chair, sat quietly in a corner, unobtrusive but alert.

With something of a bustling air the coroner came in. Coroner Benson was a fussy sort of man, with a somewhat exaggerated sense of his own importance.

He paused with what he probably considered a dramatic start when he saw the dead body of Miss Van Norman, and, shaking his head, said, "Alas! Alas!" in tragic tones.

Miss Morton and Kitty French had followed him in, and stood arm in arm, a little bewildered, but determined to know whatever might transpire. Cicely Dupuy and Miss Markham had also come in.

But after a glance round and a preliminary clearing of his throat, he at once requested that everybody except the two doctors should leave the room.

Fessenden and Kitty French were greatly disappointed at this, but the others went out with a feeling of relief, for the strain was beginning to tell upon the nerves of all concerned.

As usual, Miss Morton tried to exercise her powers of generalship, and directed that they should all assemble in the drawing-room until recalled to learn the coroner's opinion.

Mrs. Markham, unheeding Miss Morton's dictum, went away to attend to her household duties, and Cicely went to her own room, but the others waited in the drawing-room. They were joined shortly by Tom Willard and Schuyler Carleton, who arrived at about the same time.

Mr. Carleton, never a robust man, looked like a wreck of his former self. Years had been added to his apparent age; his impassive face wore a look of stony grief, and his dark eyes seemed filled with an unutterable horror.

Tom Willard, on the contrary, being of stout build and rubicund countenance, seemed an ill-fitting figure in the sad and tearful group.

But as Kitty French remarked to Fessenden in a whisper, "Poor Tom probably feels the worst of any of us, and it isn't his fault that he can't make that fat, jolly face of his look more funereal."

"And he's said to be the heir to the estate, too," Fessenden whispered back.

"Now, that's mean of you," declared Kitty. "Tom hasn't a greedy hair in his head, and I don't believe he has even thought of his fortune. And, besides, he was desperately in love with Madeleine. A whole heap more in love than Mr. Carleton was."

Fessenden stared at her. "Then why was Carleton marrying her?"

"For her money," said Kitty, with a disdainful air.

"I didn't know that," went on Fessenden, quite seriously. "I thought Carleton was hard hit. She was a magnificent woman."

"Oh, she was, indeed," agreed Kitty enthusiastically. "Mr. Carleton didn't half appreciate her, and Tom did. But then she was always very different with Tom. Somehow she always seemed constrained when with Mr. Carleton."

"Then why was she marrying him?"

"She was terribly in love with him. She liked Tom only in a cousinly way, but she adored Mr. Carleton. I know it."

"Well, it seems you were right about her not killing herself, so you're probably right about this matter, too."

"Now, that shows a nice spirit," said Kitty, smiling, even in the midst of her sorrow. "But, truly, I'm 'most always right; aren't you?"

"I shall be after this, for I'm always going to agree with you."

"That's a pretty large order, for I'm sometimes awfully disagreeable."

"I shouldn't believe that, but I've practically promised to believe everything you tell me, so I suppose I shall have to."

"Oh, now I have defeated my own ends! Well, never mind;

40

abide by your first impression,—that I'm always right,—and then go ahead."

"Go ahead it is," declared Fessenden, and then Molly Gardner joined them. Molly was more overcome by the tragic turn affairs had taken than Kitty, and had only just made her appearance downstairs that day.

"You dear child," cried Kitty, noting her pale cheeks and sad eyes, "sit right down here by us, and let Mr. Fessenden talk to you. He's the nicest man in the world to cheer any one up."

"And you look as if you need cheering, Miss Gardner," said Fessenden, arranging some pillows at her back, as she languidly dropped down on the sofa.

"I can't realize it at all," said poor Molly; "I don't want to be silly and keep fainting all over the place, but every time I remember how Maddy looked last night——" She glanced toward the closed library doors with a shudder.

"Don't think about it," said Rob Fessenden gently. "What you need most, Miss Gardner, is a bit of fresh air. Come with me for a little walk in the grounds."

This was self-sacrifice on the part of the young man, for he greatly desired to be present when the coroner should open the closed doors to them again. But he really thought Miss Gardner would be better for a short, brisk walk, and, getting her some wraps, they went out at the front door.

VII

MR. BENSON'S QUESTIONS

It was some time after Fessenden and Molly had returned from their walk that the library doors were thrown open, and Coroner Benson invited them all to come in.

They filed in slowly, each heart heavy with an impending sense of dread. Doctor Hills ushered them to seats, which had been arranged in rows, and which gave an unpleasantly formal air to the cozy library.

The body of Madeleine Van Norman had been taken upstairs to her own room, and at the library table, where she had last sat, stood Coroner Benson.

The women were seated in front. Mrs. Markham seemed to have settled into a sort of sad apathy, but Miss Morton was briskly alert and, though evidently nervous, seemed eager to hear what the coroner had to tell.

Kitty French, too, was full of anxious interest, and, taking the seat assigned to her, clasped her little hands in breathless suspense, while a high color rose to her lovely cheeks.

Molly Gardner was pale and wan-looking. She dreaded the whole scene, and had but one desire, to get away from Mapleton. She could have gone to her room, had she chosen, but the idea of being all alone was even worse than the present conditions. So she sat, with overwrought nerves, now and then clutching at Kitty's sleeve.

Cicely Dupuy was very calm—so calm, indeed, that one might guess it was the composure of an all-compelling determination, and by no means the quiet of indifference.

Marie was there, and showed the impassive face of the well-trained servant, though her volatile French nature was discernible in her quick-darting glances and quivering, sensitive lips.

The two doctors, Mr. Carlton, Tom Willard, and young Fessenden occupied the next row of seats, and behind them were the house servants.

Unlike the women, the men showed little or no emotion on their faces. All were grave and composed, and even Doctor Leonard seemed to have laid aside his brusque and aggressive ways.

As he stood facing this group, Coroner Benson was fully alive to the importance of his own position, and he quite consciously

42

determined to conduct the proceedings in a way to throw great credit upon himself in his official capacity.

After an impressive pause, which he seemed to deem necessary to gain the attention of an already breathlessly listening audience, he began:

"While there is much evidence that seems to prove that Miss Van Norman took her own life, there is very grave reason to doubt this. Both of the eminent physicians here present are inclined to believe that the dagger thrust which killed Miss Van Norman was not inflicted by her own hand, though it may have been so. This conclusion they arrive at from their scientific knowledge of the nature and direction of dagger strokes, which, as may not be generally known, is a science in itself. Indeed, were it not for the conclusive evidence of the written paper, these gentlemen would believe that the stroke was impossible of self-infliction.

"But, aside from this point, we are confronted by this startling fact. Although the dagger, which you may see still lying on the table, has several blood-stains on its handle, there is absolutely no trace of blood on the right hand of the body of Miss Van Norman. It is inconceivable that she could have removed such a trace, had there been any, and it is highly improbable, if not indeed impossible, that she could have handled the dagger and left it in its present condition, without showing a corresponding stain on her hand."

This speech of Coroner Benson's produced a decided sensation on all his hearers, but it was manifested in various ways. Kitty French exchanged with Fessenden a satisfied nod, for this seemed in line with her own theory.

Fessenden returned the nod, and even gave Kitty a faint smile, for who could look at that lovely face without a pleasant recognition of some sort? And then he folded his arms and began to think hard. Yet there was little food for coherent thought.

Granting the logical deduction from the absence of any stain on Miss Van Norman's hands, there was, as yet, not the slightest indication of any direction in which to look for the dastard who had done the deed.

Schuyler Carleton showed no emotion, but his white face seemed to take on one more degree of horror and misery. Tom Willard looked blankly amazed, and Mrs. Markham began on a new one of her successive crying spells. Miss Morton sat bolt upright and placidly smoothed the gray silk folds of her gown, while her face wore a decided "I told you so" expression, though she hadn't told them anything of the sort.

But as Fessenden watched her—the rows of seats were slightly horseshoed, and he could see her side face well—he noticed that she

43

was really trembling all over, and that her placidity of face was without doubt assumed for effect. He could not see her eyes, but he was positive that only a strong fear or terror of something could explain her admirably suppressed agitation.

The behavior of Cicely Dupuy was perhaps the most extraordinary. She flew into a fit of violent hysterics, and had to be taken from the room. Marie followed her, as it had always been part of the French maid's duty to attend Miss Dupuy upon occasion as well as Miss Van Norman.

"In view of this state of affairs," went on the coroner, when quiet had been restored after Cicely's departure, "it becomes necessary to make an investigation of the case. We have absolutely no evidence, and no real reason to suspect foul play, yet since there is the merest possibility that the death was not a suicide, it becomes my duty to look further into the matter. I have been told that Miss Van Norman had expressed a sort of general fear that she might some day be impelled to turn this dagger upon herself. But that is a peculiar mental obsession that affects many people at sight of a sharp-pointed or cutting instrument, and is by no means a proof that she did do this thing. But quite aside from the temptation of the glittering steel, we have Miss Van Norman's written confession that she at least contemplated taking her own life, and ascribing a reason therefor. In further consideration, then, of this written paper, of which you all know the contents, can any of you tell me of any fact or quote any words spoken by Miss Van Norman that would corroborate or amplify the statement of this despairing message?"

As Mr. Benson spoke, he held in his hand the written paper that had been found on the library table. It was indeed unnecessary to read it aloud, for every one present knew its contents by heart.

But nobody responded to the coroner's question. Mr. Carleton looked mutely helpless, Tom Willard looked honestly perplexed, and yet many of those present believed that both these men knew the sad secret of Madeleine's life, and understood definitely the written message.

Again Mr. Benson earnestly requested that any one knowing the least fact, however trivial, regarding the matter, would mention it.

Then Mrs. Markham spoke.

"I can tell you nothing but my own surmise," she said; "I know nothing for certain, but I have reason to believe that Madeleine Van Norman had a deep sorrow,—such a one as would impel her to write that statement, and to act in accordance with it."

"That is what I wished to know," said Coroner Benson; "it is not necessary for you to detail the nature of her sorrow, or even to hint at it further, but the assurance that the message is in accordance with Miss Van Norman's mental attitude goes far toward convincing me that her death is the outcome of that written declaration."

"I know, too," volunteered Kitty French, "that Madeleine meant every word she wrote there. She was miserable, and for the very reason that she herself stated!"

Mr. Benson pinched his glasses more firmly on his nose, and turned his gaze slowly toward Miss French.

Kitty had spoken impulsively, and perhaps too directly, but, though embarrassed at the sensation she had caused, she showed no desire to retract her statements.

"I am told," said the coroner, his voice ringing out clearly in the strange silence that had fallen on the room, "that the initial on this paper designates Mr. Schuyler Carleton. I must therefore ask Mr. Carleton if he can explain the reference to himself."

"I cannot," said Schuyler Carleton, and only the intense silence allowed his low whisper to be heard. "Miss Van Norman was my affianced wife. We were to have been married to-day. Those two facts, I think, prove the existence of our mutual love. The paper is to me inexplicable."

Tom Willard looked at the speaker with an expression of frank unbelief, and, indeed, most of the auditors' faces betrayed incredulity.

Even with no previous reason to imagine that Carleton did not love Madeleine, the tragic message proved it beyond all possible doubt,—and yet it was but natural for the man to deny it.

Doctor Hills spoke next.

"I think, Coroner Benson," he said, as he rose to his feet, "we are missing the point. If Miss Van Norman took her life in fulfilment of her own decision, the reasons that brought about that decision are not a matter for our consideration. It is for us to decide whether she did or did not bring about her own death, and as a mode of procedure may I suggest this? Doctor Leonard and myself hold, that, in view of the absence of any stain on Miss Van Norman's hands, she could not have handled the stained dagger that killed her. A refutation of this opinion would be to explain how she could have done the deed and left no trace on her fingers. Unless this can be shown, I think we can not call it a suicide."

Although nothing would have induced him to admit it, Coroner Benson was greatly accommodated by this suggestion, and immediately adopting it as his own promulgation, he repeated it almost exactly word for word, as his official dictum.

"And so," he concluded, "as I have now explained, unless a

theory can be offered on this point, we must agree that Miss Van Norman's unfortunate death was not by her own hand."

Robert Fessenden arose.

"I have no theory," he said; "I have no argument to offer. But I am sure we all wish to discover the truth by means of any light that any of us may throw on the mystery. And I want to say that in my opinion the absence of blood on the hands, though it indicates, does not positively prove, that the weapon was held by another than the victim. Might it not be that, taking the dagger from the table, clean as of course it was, Miss Van Norman turned it upon herself, and then, withdrawing it, let it drop to the floor, where it subsequently became blood-stained, as did the rug and her own gown?"

The two doctors listened intently. It was characteristic of both that though Doctor Hills had shown no elation when he had convinced Doctor Leonard of his mistake the night before, yet now Doctor Leonard could not repress a gleam of triumph in his eyes as he turned to Doctor Hills.

"It is possible," said Mr. Benson, with a cautiously dubious air, though really the theory struck him as extremely probable, and he wished he had advanced it himself.

Doctor Hills looked thoughtful, and then, as nobody else spoke, he observed:

"Mr. Carleton might perhaps judge of that point. As he first discovered the dagger, and picked it up from the floor, he can perhaps say if it lay in or near the stains on the carpet."

Everybody looked at Schuyler Carleton. But the man had reached the limit of his endurance.

"I don't know!" he exclaimed, covering his white face with his hands, as if to shut out the awful memory. "Do you suppose I noticed such details?" he cried, looking up again. "I picked up the dagger, scarce knowing that I did it! It was almost an unconscious act. I was stunned, dazed, at what I saw before me, and I know nothing of the dagger or its blood-stains!"

Truly, the man was almost frenzied, and out of consideration for his perturbed state, the coroner asked him no more questions just then.

"It seems to me," observed Rob Fessenden, "that the nature or shape of the stains on the dagger handle might determine this point. If they appear to be finger-marks, the weapon must have been held by some other hand. If merely stains, as from the floor, they might be considered to strengthen Doctor Hill's theory."

The Venetian paper-cutter was produced and passed around.

None of the women would touch it or even look at it, except Kitty French. She examined it carefully, but had no opinion to offer,

46

and Mr. Benson waited impatiently for her to finish her scrutiny. He had no wish to hear her remarks on the subject, for he deemed her a mere frivolous girl, who had no business to take any part in the serious inquiry. All were requested not to touch the weapon, which was passed round on a brass tray taken from the library table.

Schuyler Carleton covered his eyes, and refused to glance at it.

Tom Willard and Robert Fessenden looked at it at the same time, holding the tray between them.

"I make out no finger-prints," said Tom, at last. "Do you?"

"No," said Fessenden; "that is, not surely. These may be marks of fingers, but they are far too indistinct to say so positively. What do you think, Doctor Leonard?"

The gruesome property was passed on to the two doctors, who examined it with the greatest care. Going to the window, they looked at it with magnifying glasses, and finally reported that the slight marks might be finger-marks, or might be the abrasion of the nap of the rug on which the dagger had fallen.

"Then," said Coroner Benson, "we have, so far, no evidence which refutes the theory that Miss Van Norman's written message was the expression of her deliberate intent, and that that intention was fulfilled by her."

Once more Mr. Benson scanned intently the faces of his audience.

"Can no one, then," he said again, "assert or suggest anything that may have any bearing on this written message?"

"I can," said Robert Fessenden.

VIII

A SOFT LEAD PENCIL

Coroner Benson looked at the young man curiously. Knowing him to be a stranger in the household, he had not expected information from him.

"Your name?" he said quietly.

"I am Robert Fessenden, of New York City. I am a lawyer by profession, and I came to Mapleton yesterday for the purpose of acting as best man at Mr. Carleton's wedding. I came here this morning, not knowing of what had occurred in the night, and after conversation with some members of the household I felt impelled to investigate some points which seemed to me mysterious. I trust I have shown no intrusive curiosity, but I confess to a natural detective instinct, and I noticed some peculiarities about that paper you hold in your hand to which I should like to call your attention."

Fessenden's words caused a decided stir among his hearers, including the coroner and the two doctors.

Mr. Benson was truly anxious to learn what the young man had to say, but at the same time his professional jealousy was aroused by the implication that there was anything to be learned from the paper itself, outside of his own information concerning it.

"I was told," he said quickly, "that this paper is positively written in Miss Van Norman's own hand."

Robert Fessenden, while not exactly a handsome man, was of a type that impressed every one pleasantly. He was large and blond, and had an air that was unmistakably cultured and exceedingly well-bred. Conventionality sat well upon him, and his courteous self-assurance had in it no trace of egotism or self-importance. In a word, he was what the plain-spoken people of Mapleton called citified, and though they sometimes resented this combination of personal traits, in their hearts they admired and envied it.

This was why Coroner Benson felt a slight irritation at the young man's savoir faire, and at the same time a sense of satisfaction that there was promise of some worth-while help.

"I was told so, too," said Fessenden, in response to the coroner's remark, "and as I have never seen any of Miss Van Norman's writing, I have, of course, no reason to doubt this. But this is the point I want to inquire about: is it assumed that Miss Van Norman wrote the words on this paper while sitting here at the table last evening, immediately or shortly before her death?"

Mr. Benson thought a moment, then he said: "Without any evidence to the contrary, and indeed without having given this question any previous thought, I think I may say that it has been tacitly assumed that this is a dying confession of Miss Van Norman's."

He looked inquiringly at his audience, and Doctor Hills responded.

"Yes," he said; "we have taken for granted that Miss Van Norman wrote the message while sitting here last evening, after the rest of the household had retired. This we infer from the fact of Mr. Carleton's finding the paper on the table when he discovered the tragedy."

"You thought the same, Mr. Carleton?"

"Of course; I could not do otherwise than to believe Miss Van Norman had written the message and had then carried out her resolve."

"I think, Mr. Fessenden," resumed the coroner, "we may assume this to be the case."

"Then," said Fessenden, "I will undertake to show that it is improbable that this paper was written as has been supposed. The message is, as you see, written in pencil. The pencil here on the table, and which is part of a set of desk-fittings, is a very hard pencil, labeled H. A few marks made by it upon a bit of paper will convince you at once that it is not the pencil which was used to write that message. The letters, as you see, are formed of heavy black marks which were made with a very soft pencil, such as is designated by 2 B or BB. If you please, I will pause for a moment while you satisfy yourself upon this point."

Greatly interested, Mr. Benson took the pencil from the pen-rack and wrote some words upon a pad of paper. Doctor Leonard and Doctor Hills leaned over the table to note results, but no one else stirred.

"You are quite right," said Mr. Benson; "this message was not written with this pencil. But what does that prove?"

"It proves nothing," said Fessenden calmly, "but it is pretty strong evidence that the message was not written at this table last night. For had there been any other pencil on the table, it would doubtless have remained. Assuming, then that Miss Van Norman wrote this message elsewhere, and with another pencil, it loses the special importance commonly attributed to the words of one about to die."

"It does," said Mr. Benson, impressed by the fact, but at a loss to know whither the argument was leading.

"Believing, then," went on the lawyer, "that this paper had not

49

been written in this room last evening, I began to conjecture where it had been written. For one would scarcely expect a message of that nature to be written in one place and carried to another. I was so firmly convinced that something could be learned on this point, that just before we were summoned to this room, I asked permission of Mrs. Markham to examine the appointments of Miss Van Norman's writing-desk in her own room, and I found in her desk no soft pencils whatever. There were several pencils, of gold and of silver and of ordinary wood, but the lead in each was as hard as this one on the library table. Urged on by what seemed to me important developments, I persuaded Mrs. Markham to let me examine all of the writing-desks in the house. I found but one soft pencil, and that was in the desk of Miss Dupuy, Miss Van Norman's secretary. It is quite conceivable that Miss Van Norman should write at her secretary's desk, but I found myself suddenly confronted by another disclosure. And that is that the handwritings of Miss Van Norman and Miss Dupuy are so similar as to be almost identical. In view of the importance of this written message, should it not be more carefully proved that this writing is really Miss Van Norman's own?"

"It should, indeed," declared Coroner Benson, who was by this time quite ready to agree to any suggestion Mr. Fessenden might make. "Will somebody please ask Miss Dupuy to come here?"

"I will," said Miss Morton, and, rising, she quickly rustled from the room.

Of course, every one present immediately remembered that Miss Dupuy had left the room in a fit of hysterical emotion, and wondered in what frame of mind she would return.

Nearly every one, too, resented Miss Morton's officiousness. Whatever errand was to be done, she volunteered to do it, quite as if she were a prominent member of the household, instead of a lately arrived guest.

"This similarity of penmanship is a very important point," observed Mr. Benson, "a very important point indeed. I am surprised that it has not been remarked sooner."

"I've often noticed that they wrote alike," said Kitty French impulsively, "but I never thought about it before in this matter. You see"—she involuntarily addressed herself to the coroner, who listened with interest—"you see, Madeleine instructed Cicely to write as nearly as possible like she did, because Cicely was her social secretary and answered all her notes, and wrote letters for her, and sometimes Cicely signed Madeleine's name to the notes, and the people who received them thought Maddy wrote them herself. She didn't mean to deceive, only sometimes people don't like to have their notes answered by a secretary, and so it saved a lot of trouble. I

50

confess," Kitty concluded, "that I can't always tell the difference in their writing myself, though I usually can."

Miss Morton returned, bringing Cicely with her. Still officious of manner, Miss Morton rearranged some chairs, and then seated herself in the front row with Cicely beside her. She showed what seemed almost an air of proprietorship in the girl, patting her shoulder, and whispering to her, as if by way of encouragement.

But Miss Dupuy's demeanor had greatly changed. No longer weeping, she had assumed an almost defiant attitude, and her thin lips were tightly closed in a way that did not look promising to those who desired information.

With a conspicuous absence of tact or diplomacy, Mr. Benson asked her abruptly, "Did you write this paper?"

"I did," said Cicely, and as soon as the words were uttered her lips closed again with a snap.

Her reply fell like a bombshell upon the breathless group of listeners. Tom Willard was the first to speak.

"What!" he exclaimed. "Maddy didn't write that? You wrote it?"

"Yes," asserted Cicely, looking Tom squarely in the eyes.

"When did you write it?" asked the coroner.

"A week or more ago."

"Why did you write it?"

"I refuse to tell."

"Who is the S. mentioned on this paper?"

"I refuse to tell."

"You needn't tell. That is outside the case. It is sufficient for us to know that Miss Van Norman did not write this paper. If you wrote it, it has no bearing on the case. Your penmanship is very like hers."

"I practised to make it so," said Cicely. "Miss Van Norman desired me to do so, that I might answer unimportant notes and sign her name to them. They were in no sense forgeries. Ladies frequently have their own names signed by their secretaries. Miss Van Norman often received notes like that."

"Why did you not tell before that you wrote this paper supposed to have been written by Miss Van Norman?"

"Nobody asked me." Miss Dupuy's tone was defiant and even pert. Robert Fessenden began to look at the girl with increasing interest. He felt quite sure that she knew more about the tragedy than he had suspected. His detective instinct became immediately alert, and he glanced significantly at Kitty French.

She was breathlessly watching Cicely, but nothing could be learned from the girl's inscrutable face, and to an attentive listener her very voice did not ring true.

51

Doctor Leonard and Doctor Hills looked at each other. Both remembered that the night before, Cicely had stealthily opened the door of the library and put her head in, but seeing them, had quickly gone back again.

This information might or might not be of importance, but after a brief whispered conference, the two men concluded that it was not the time then to refer to it.

Mr. Carleton, though still pale and haggard of face, seemed to have taken on new interest, and listened attentively to the conversation, while big, good-natured Tom Willard leaned forward and took the paper, and then sat studying it, with a perplexed expression.

"But why did you not volunteer the information? You must have known it was of great importance." The coroner spoke almost petulantly, and indeed Miss Dupuy had suppressed important information.

At his question she became greatly embarrassed. She blushed and looked down, and then, with an effort resuming her air of defiance, she snapped out her answer: "I was afraid."

"Afraid of what?"

"Afraid that they would think somebody killed Miss Van Norman, instead of that she killed herself, as she did."

"How do you know she did?"

"I don't know it, except that I left her here alone when I went to my room, and the house was all locked up, and soon after that she was found dead. So she must have killed herself."

"Those conclusions," said the coroner pompously, "are for us to arrive at, not for you to declare. The case," he then said, turning toward the doctors and the young detective, "is entirely changed by the hearing of Miss Dupuy's testimony. The fact that the note was not written by Miss Van Norman, will, I'm sure, remove from the minds of the doctors the possibility of suicide."

"It certainly will," said Doctor Leonard. "I quite agree with Doctor Hills that except for the note all evidence is against the theory of suicide."

"Then," went on Mr. Benson, "if it is not a suicide, Miss Van Norman must have been the victim of foul play, and it is our duty to investigate the matter, and attempt to discover whose hand it was that wielded the fatal dagger."

Mr. Benson was fond of high-sounding words and phrases, and, finding himself in charge of what promised to be a mysterious, if not a celebrated, case, he made the most of his authoritative position.

Robert Fessenden paid little attention to the coroner's speech. His brain was working rapidly, and he was trying to piece together such data as he had already accumulated in the way of evidence. It was but little, to be sure, and in lieu of definite clues he allowed himself to speculate a little on the probabilities.

But he realized that he was in the presence of a mysterious murder case, and he was more than willing to do anything he could toward discovering the truth of the matter.

The known facts were so appalling, and any evidence of undiscovered facts was as yet so extremely slight, that Fessenden felt there was a great deal to be done.

He was trying to collect and systematize his own small fund of information when he realized that the audience was being dismissed.

Mr. Benson announced that he would convene a jury and hold an inquest that same afternoon, and then he would expect all those now present to return as witnesses.

Without waiting to learn what the others did, Fessenden turned to Kitty French, and asked her to go with him for a stroll.

"You need fresh air," he said, as they stepped from the veranda; "but, also, I need you to talk to. I can formulate my ideas better if I express them aloud, and you are such a clear-headed and sympathetic listener that it helps a lot."

Kitty smiled with pleasure at the compliment, then her pretty face became grave again as she remembered what must be the subject of their conversation.

"Before I talk to the lawyers or detectives who will doubtless soon infest the house, I want to straighten out my own ideas."

"I don't see how you can have any," said Kitty; "I mean, of course, any definite ideas about who committed the murder."

"I haven't really definite ones, but I want you to help me get some."

"Well," said Kitty, looking provokingly lovely in her serious endeavor to be helpful, "let's sit down here and talk it over."

"Here" was a sort of a rustic arbor, which was a delightful place for a tête-à-tête, but not at all conducive to deep thought or profound conversation.

"Go on," said Kitty, pursing her red lips and puckering her white brow in her determination to supply the help that was required of her.

"But I can't go on, if you look like that! All logic and deduction fly out of my head, and I can think only of poetry and romance. And it won't do! At least, not now. Can't you try to give a more successful imitation of a coroner's jury?"

Kitty tried to look stupid and wise, both at once, and only succeeded in looking bewitching.

"It's no use," said Fessenden; "I can't sit facing you, as I would the real thing in the way of juries. So I'll sit beside you, and look at the side of that distant barn, while we talk."

So he turned partly round, and, fixing his gaze on the stolid red barn, said abruptly:

"Who wrote that paper?"

"I don't know," said Kitty, feeling that she couldn't help much here.

"Somehow, I can't seem to believe that Dupuy girl wrote it. She sounded to me like a lady reciting a fabrication."

"I thought that, too," said Kitty. "I never liked Cicely, because I never trusted her. But Maddy was very fond of her, and she wouldn't have been, unless she had found Cicely trustworthy."

"Come to luncheon, you two," said Tom Willard, as he approached the arbor.

"Oh, Mr. Willard," said Kitty, "who do you think wrote that paper?"

"Why, Miss Dupuy," said Tom, in surprise. "She owned up to it."

"Yes, I know; but I'm not sure she told the truth."

"I don't know why she shouldn't," said Tom, thoughtfully. And then he added gently, "And, after looking at it closely, I felt sure, myself, it wasn't Maddy's writing, after all."

"Then it must be Cicely's," said Kitty. "I admit I can't tell them apart."

And then the three went back to the house.

IX

THE WILL

Immediately after luncheon Lawyer Peabody came. This gentleman had had charge of the Van Norman legal matters for many years, and it was known by most of those present that he was bringing with him such wills or other documents as might have a bearing on the present crisis.

Mr. Peabody was an old man; moreover, he had for many years been intimately associated with the Van Norman household, and had been a close friend of both Richard Van Norman and Madeleine. Shattered and broken by the sad tragedy in the household, he could scarcely repress his emotion when he undertook to address the little audience.

But the main purport of his business there at that time was to announce the contents of the two wills in his possession.

The first one, the will of Richard Van Norman, was no surprise to any one present, except perhaps those few who did not live in Mapleton. One of these, Robert Fessenden, was extremely interested to learn that because of Madeleine's death before her marriage, and also before she was twenty-three years of age, the large fortune of Richard Van Norman, which would have been hers on her wedding day, passed at once and unrestrictedly to Tom Willard.

But also by the terms of Richard Van Norman's will the fine old mansion and grounds and a sum of money, modest in comparison with the whole fortune, but ample to maintain the estate, were Madeleine's own, and had been from the day of her uncle's death.

Possessed of this property, therefore, Madeleine had made a will which was dated a few months before her death, and which Mr. Peabody now read.

After appropriate and substantial bequests to several intimate friends, to her housekeeper and secretary, and to all the servants, Madeleine devised that her residuary fortune and the Van Norman house and grounds should become the property of Miss Elizabeth Morton.

This was a complete surprise to all, with the possible exception of Miss Morton herself. It was not easy to judge from her haughty and self-satisfied countenance whether she had known of this before or not.

Fessenden, who was watching her closely, was inclined to think

55

she had known of it, and again his busy imagination ran riot. The first point, he thought to himself, in discovering a potential murderer, is to inquire who will be benefited by the victim's death. Apparently the only ones to profit by the passing of Madeleine Van Norman were Tom Willard and Miss Morton. But even the ingenious imagination of the young detective balked at the idea of connecting either of these two with the tragedy. He knew Willard had not been in the house at the time of the murder, and Miss Morton, as he had chanced to discover, had occupied a room on the third floor. Moreover, it was absurd on the face of things to fancy a well-bred, middle-aged lady stealing downstairs at dead of night to kill her charming young hostess!

It was with a sense of satisfaction therefore that Fessenden assured himself that he had formed no suspicions whatever, and could listen with a mind entirely unprejudiced to such evidence as the coroner's inquiry might bring forth.

He was even glad that he had not discussed the matter further with Kitty French. He still thought she had clear vision and good judgment, but he had begun to realize that in her presence his own clearness of vision was dazzled by her dancing eyes and a certain distracting charm which he had never before observed in any woman.

But he told himself somewhat sternly that feminine charm must not be allowed to interfere with the present business in hand, and he seated himself at a considerable distance from Kitty French, when it was time for the inquest.

A slight delay was occasioned by waiting for Coroner Benson's own stenographer, but when he arrived the inquiry was at once begun.

At the request of Miss Morton, or, it might rather be said, at her command, the whole assembly had moved to the drawing-room, it being a much larger and more airy apartment, and withal less haunted by the picture of the tragedy itself.

And yet to hold a coroner's inquiry in a room gay with wedding decorations was almost, if not quite, as ghastly.

But Coroner Benson paid no heed to emotional considerations and conducted himself with the same air of justice and legality as if he had been in a court-room or the town-hall.

As for the jury he had gathered, the half-dozen men, though filled with righteous indignation at the crime committed in their village, wasted no thought on the incongruity of their surroundings.

Coroner Benson put his first question to Mrs. Markham, as he considered her, in a way at least, the present head of the household. To be sure, the house now legally belonged to Miss Morton, and that

56

lady was quickly assuming an added air of importance which was doubtless the result of her recent inheritance; but Mrs. Markham was still housekeeper, and by virtue of her long association with the place, Mr. Benson chose to treat her with exceeding courtesy and deference.

But Mrs. Markham, though now quite composed and willing to answer questions, could give no evidence of any importance. She testified that she had seen Madeleine last at about ten o'clock the night before. This was after the guests who had been at dinner had gone away, and the house guests had gone to their rooms. Miss Van Norman was alone in the library, and as Mrs. Markham left her she asked her to send Cicely Dupuy to the library. Mrs. Markham had then gone directly to her own room, which was on the second floor, above the drawing-room. It was at the front of the house, and the room behind it, also over the long drawing-room, was the one now devoted to the exhibition of Madeleine's wedding gifts. Mrs. Markham had retired almost immediately and had heard no unusual sounds. She explained, however, that she was somewhat deaf, and had there been any disturbance downstairs it was by no means probable that she would have heard it.

"What was the first intimation you had that anything had happened?" asked Mr. Benson.

"Kitty French came to my door and called to me. Her excited voice made me think something was wrong, and, dressing hastily, I came downstairs, to find many of the household already assembled."

"And then you went into the library?"

"Yes; I had no idea Madeleine was dead. I thought she had fainted, and I went toward her at once."

"Did you touch her?"

"Yes; and I saw at once she was not living, but Miss Morton said perhaps she might be, and then she telephoned for Doctor Hills."

"Can you tell me if the house is carefully locked at night?"

"It is, I am sure; but it is not in my province to attend to it."

"Whose duty is it?"

"That of Harris, the butler."

"Will you please call Harris at once?" Mr. Benson's tone of finality seemed to dismiss Mrs. Markham as a witness, and she rang the bell for the butler.

Harris came in, a perfect specimen of that type of butler that is so similar to a certain type of bishop.

Aside from the gravity of the occasion, he seemed to show a separate gravity of position, of importance, and of all-embracing knowledge.

57

"Your name is Harris?" said Mr. Benson.

"Yes, sir; James Harris, sir."

"You have been employed in this house for some years?"

"Seventeen years and more, sir."

"Is it your duty to lock up the house at night?"

"It is, sir. Mr. Van Norman was most particular about it, sir, being as how the house is alone like in the grounds, and there being so much trees and shrubberies about."

"There are strong bolts to doors and windows?"

"Most especial strong, sir. It was Mr. Van Norman's wish to make it impossible for burglars to get in."

"And did he succeed in this?"

"He did, sir, for sure. There are patent locks on every door and window, more than one on most of them; and whenever Mr. Van Norman heard of a new kind of lock, he'd order it at once."

"Is the house fitted with burglar alarms?"

"No, sir; Mr. Van Norman depended on his safety locks and strong bolts. He said he didn't want no alarm, because it was forever getting out o' kilter, and bolts were surer, after all."

"And every night you make sure that these bolts and fastenings are all secured in place?"

"I do, sir, and I have done it for many years."

"You looked after them last night, as usual?"

"Sure, sir; every one of them I attended to myself."

"You can testify, then, that the house could not have been entered by a burglar last night?" asked Mr. Benson.

"Not by a burglar, nor by nobody else, sir, unless they broke down a door or cut out a pane of glass."

"Yet Mr. Carleton came in."

Harris looked annoyed. "Of course, sir, anybody could come in the front door with a latch-key. I didn't mean that they couldn't. But all the other doors and windows were fastened all right, and I found them all right this morning."

"You made a careful examination of them?"

"Yes, sir. Of course we was all up through the night, and as soon as I learned that Miss Madeleine was—was gone, sir, I felt I ought to look about a bit. And everything was as right as could be, sir. No burglar was into this house last night, sir."

"How about the cellar?"

"We never bother much about the cellar, sir, as there's nothing down there to steal, unless they take the furnace or the gas-meter. But the door at the top of the cellar stairs, as opens into the hall, sir, is locked every night with a double lock and a bolt besides."

"Then no burglar could come up through the cellar way?"

58

"That he couldn't, sir. Nor yet down through the skylight, for the skylight is bolted every night same as the windows."

"And the windows on the second floor—are they fastened at night?"

"They are in the halls, sir. But of course in the bedrooms I don't know how they may be. That is, the occupied bedrooms. When the guest rooms are vacant I always fasten those windows."

"Then you can testify, Harris, that there was no way for any one to enter this house last night except at the front door with a latch-key or through the window of some occupied bedroom?"

"I can swear to that, sir."

"You are sure you've overlooked no way? No back window, or seldom-used door?"

Harris was a little hurt at this insistent questioning, but the coroner recognized that this was a most important bit of evidence, and so pressed his questions.

"I'm sure of it, sir. Mr. Van Norman taught me to be most thorough about this matter, and I've never done different since Miss Madeleine has been mistress here."

"That is all, thank you, Harris. You may go."

Harris went away, his honest countenance showing a look of relief that his ordeal was over, and yet betokening a perplexed anxiety also.

Cicely Dupuy was next called upon to give her evidence, or rather to continue the testimony which she had begun in the library. The girl had a pleasanter expression than she had shown at the previous questioning, but a red spot burned in either cheek, and she was clearly trying to be calm, though really under stress of a great excitement.

"You were with Miss Van Norman in the library last evening?" began Mr. Benson, speaking more gently than he had been doing, for he feared an emotional outburst might again render this witness unavailable.

"Yes," said Miss Dupuy, in a low tone; "when Mrs. Markham came upstairs she stopped at my door and said Miss Van Norman wanted me, and I went down immediately."

"You have been Miss Van Norman's secretary for some time?"

"For nearly five years."

"What were your duties?"

"I attended to her social correspondence; helped her with her accounts, both household and personal; read to her, and often did errands and made calls for her."

"She was kind to you?"

59

"She was more than kind. She treated me always as her social equal, and as her friend."

Cicely's blue eyes filled with tears, and her voice quivered as she spoke this tribute to her employer.

Again Mr. Benson feared she would break down, and changed his course of questioning.

"At what time did you go to the library last evening?"

"It could not have been more than a few minutes past ten."

"What did you do there?"

"Miss Van Norman dictated some lists of matters to be attended to, and she discussed with me a few final arrangements for her wedding."

"Did she seem about as usual in her manner?"

"Yes,—except that she was very tired, and seemed a little preoccupied."

"And then she dismissed you?"

"Yes. She told me to go to bed, and said that she should sit up for an hour or so, and would write some notes herself."

"Apparently she did not do so, as no notes have been found in the library."

"That must be so, sir."

But as she said this, a change came over Miss Dupuy's face. She seemed to think that the absence of those notes was of startling importance, and though she tried not to show her agitation, it was clearly evident from the way she bit her lower lip, and clenched her fingers.

"At what time did Miss Van Norman dismiss you?" asked Mr. Benson, seeming to ignore her embarrassment.

"At half-past ten."

"Did you retire at once?"

"No; I had some notes to write for Miss Van Norman, and also some of my own, and I sat at my desk for some time. I don't know just how long."

"And then what happened?"

At this question Cicely Dupuy became more nervous and embarrassed than ever. She hesitated and then made two or three attempts to speak, each one of which resulted in no intelligible sound.

X

SOME TESTIMONY

"There is nothing to fear," said Mr. Benson kindly. "Simply tell us what you heard while sitting there writing, that caused you to leave your room."

Glancing around as if in search of some one, Cicely finally managed to make an audible reply. "I heard a loud cry," she said, "that sounded as if somebody were frightened or in danger. I naturally ran out into the hall, and, looking over the baluster, I saw Mr. Carleton in the hall below. I felt sure then that it was he who had cried out, so I came downstairs."

"At what time was this?"

"At half-past eleven exactly."

"How do you know so accurately?"

"Because as I came downstairs the old clock on the middle landing chimed the half-hour. It has a deep soft note, and it struck just as I passed the clock, and it startled me a little, so of course I remember it perfectly."

"And then?"

"And then"—Cicely again hesitated, but with a visible effort resumed her speech—"why, and then I came on down, and found Mr. Carleton nearly distracted. I could not guess what was the matter. He was turning on the lights and ringing the servants' bells and acting like a man beside himself. Then in a moment Marie appeared, and gave one of her French shrieks that completely upset what little nerve I had left."

"And what did you do next?"

"I—I went into the library."

"Why?"

Cicely looked up suddenly, as if startled, but after only an instant's hesitation replied:

"Because Mr. Carleton pointed toward the doorway, and Marie and I went in together."

"You knew at once that Miss Van Norman was not alive?"

"I was not sure, but Marie went toward her, and then turned away with another of her horrid screams, and I felt that Miss Van Norman must be dead."

"What did Mr. Carleton say?"

"He said nothing. He—he pointed to the written paper on the table."

61

"Which you had written yourself?"

"Yes, but he didn't know that." Cicely spoke eagerly, as if saying something of importance. "He thought she wrote it."

"Never mind that point for the moment. But I must now ask you to explain that written message which you have declared that you yourself wrote."

At this Cicely's manner changed. She became again the obstinate and defiant woman who had answered the coroner's earlier questions.

"I refuse to explain it."

"Consider a moment," said Mr. Benson quietly. "Sooner or later—perhaps at a trial—you will be obliged to explain this matter. How much better, then, to confide in us now, and perhaps lead to an immediate solution of the mystery."

Cicely pondered a moment, then she said, "I have nothing to conceal, I will tell you. I did write that paper, and it was the confession of my heart. I am very miserable, and when I wrote it I quite intended to take my own life. When I was called to go to Miss Van Norman in the library, I gathered up some notes and lists from my desk to take to her. In my haste I must have included that paper without knowing it, for when I reached my room I could not find it. And then—then when I saw it—there on the table—I——" Cicely had again grown nervous and excited. Her voice trembled, her eyes filled with tears, and, fearing a nervous collapse, Mr. Benson hurried on to other questions.

"Whom does that S. in your note stand for."

"That I shall never tell." The determination in her voice convinced him that it was useless to insist on that point, so the coroner went on.

"Perhaps we have no right to ask. Now you must tell me some other things, and, believe me, my questions are not prompted by curiosity, but are necessary to the discovery of the truth. Why did Mr. Carleton point to that paper?"

"He—he seemed so shocked and stunned that he was almost unable to speak. I suppose he thought that would explain why she had killed herself."

"But she hadn't killed herself."

"But he thought she had, and he thought that paper proved it."

"But why had he need to prove it, and to you?"

"I don't know. I don't know what he thought! I don't know what I thought myself after I reached the library door and looked in and saw that dreadful sight! Oh, I shall see it all my life!" At the memory Cicely broke down again and sank into her chair, shaking with convulsive sobs.

Mr. Benson did not disturb her further, but proceeded to question the others.

The account of Marie, the maid, merely served to corroborate what Cicely had said. Marie, too, had heard Carleton's cry for help, and, throwing on a dressing-gown, had run down-stairs to Madeleine's room. Not finding her mistress there, she had hurried down to the first floor, reaching the lower hall but a few minutes after Cicely did. She said also that it was just about half-past eleven by the clock in her own room when she heard Mr. Carleton's cry.

"You knew who it was that had called out so loudly?" asked Mr. Benson.

"No, m'sieu; I heard only the shriek as of one in great disaster. I ran to Miss Van Norman's room, as that was my first duty."

"Were you not in attendance upon her?"

"No; she had sent me the message by Miss Dupuy, that I need not attend her when she retired."

"Did this often occur?"

"Not often; but sometimes when Miss Van Norman sat up late, by herself, she would excuse me at an earlier hour. She was most kind and considerate of everybody."

"Then when at last you saw Miss Van Norman in the library, what did you do?"

"Mon Dieu! I shrieked! Why not? I was amazed, shocked, but, above all, desolated! It was a cruel scene. I knew not what to do, so, naturally, I shrieked."

Marie's French shrug almost convinced her hearers that truly that was the only thing to do on such an occasion.

"And now," said Coroner Benson, "can you tell us of anything, any incident or any knowledge of your own, that will throw any light on this whole matter?"

Marie's pretty face took on a strange expression. It was not fear or terror, but a sort of perplexity. She gave a furtive glance at Mr. Carleton and then at Miss Morton, and hesitated.

At last she spoke, slowly:

"If monsieur could perhaps word his question a little differently—with more of a definiteness——"

"Very well; do you know anything of Miss Van Norman's private affairs that would assist us in discovering who killed her."

"No, monsieur," said Marie promptly, and with a look of relief.

"Did Miss Van Norman ever, in the slightest way, express any intention or desire to end her life?"

"Never, monsieur."

"Do you think she was glad and happy in the knowledge of her fast-approaching wedding-day?"

"I am sure of it;" and Marie's tone was that of one who well knew whereof she spoke.

"That is all, then, for the present;" and Marie, with another sidelong, curious glance at Miss Morton, resumed her seat.

Kitty French and Molly Gardner were questioned, but they told nothing that would throw any light on the matter. They had heard the cry, and while hastily dressing had heard the general commotion in the house. They had thought it must be a fire, and not until they reached the library did they know what had really happened.

"And then," said Kitty indignantly, in conclusion of her own recital, "we were not allowed to stay with the others, but were sent to our rooms. So how can we give any evidence?"

It was plain to be seen, Miss French felt herself defrauded of an opportunity that should have been hers, but Miss Gardner was of quite a different mind. She answered in whispered monosyllables the questions put by the coroner, and as she knew no more than Kitty of the whole matter, she was not questioned much.

Robert Fessenden smiled a little at the different attitudes of the two girls. He knew Kitty was eager to hear all the exciting details, while Molly shrank from the whole subject. However, as they were such minor witnesses, the coroner paid little serious attention to them or to their statements.

Miss Morton's testimony came next. Fessenden regarded her with interest, as, composed and calm, she waited the coroner's interrogations.

She was deliberate and careful in making her replies, and it seemed to the young detective as if she knew nothing whatever about the whole affair, but was trying to imply that she knew a great deal.

"You went to your room when the others did, at about ten o'clock?" asked Mr. Benson.

"Yes, but I did not retire at once."

"Did you hear any sounds that caused you alarm?"

"No, not alarm. Curiosity, perhaps, but that is surely pardonable to a naturally timid woman in a strange house."

"Then you did hear sounds. Can you describe them?"

"I do not think they were other than those made by the servants attending to their duties. But the putting on of coal or the fastening of windows are noticeable sounds when one is not accustomed to them."

"You could discern, then, that it was the shovelling of coal or the fastening of windows that you heard?"

64

"No, I could not. My hearing is extremely acute, but as my room is on the third floor, all the sounds I heard were faint and muffled."

"Did you hear Mr. Carleton's cry for help?"

"I did, but at that distance it did not sound loud. However, I was sufficiently alarmed to open my door and step out into the hall. I had not taken off my evening gown, and, seeing bright lights downstairs, of course I immediately went down. The household was nearly all assembled when I reached the library. I saw at once what had happened, and I saw, too, that Mrs. Markham and the younger women were quite frantic with fright and excitement. I thought it my duty therefore to take up the reins of government, and I took the liberty of telephoning for the doctor. I think there is nothing more of importance that I can tell you."

At this Fessenden barely repressed a smile, for he could not see that Miss Morton had told anything of importance at all.

"I would like," said Mr. Benson, "for you to inform us as to your relations with the Van Norman household. Have you been long acquainted with Miss Van Norman?"

"About two years," replied Miss Morton, with a snapping together of her teeth, which was one of her many peculiarities of manner.

"And how did the acquaintance come about?"

"Her uncle and I were friends many years ago," said Miss Morton. "I knew Richard Van Norman before Madeleine was born. We quarrelled, and I never saw him again. After his death Madeleine wrote to me, and several letters passed between us. At her invitation I made a short visit here about a year ago. Again, at her invitation, I came here yesterday to be present at her wedding."

Miss Morton's manner, though quiet, betokened repressed excitement rather than suppressed emotion. In no way did her hard, bright eyes show grief or sorrow, but they flashed in a way that indicated high nervous pressure.

"Did you know that you were to inherit this house and a large sum of money at Miss Van Norman's death?" The question was thrown at her so suddenly that Miss Morton almost gasped.

She hesitated for an appreciable instant, then with a sudden snap of her strong, angular jaw, she said, "No!"

"You had no intimation of it whatever?"

"No." Again that excessive decision of manner, which to Fessenden's mind, at least, stultified rather than corroborated the verity of her statement.

But Coroner Benson expressed no doubt of his witness, but merely said casually:

"Yet, on the occasion of the tragedy last night, you at once

65

assumed the attitude of the head of the house. You gave orders to the servants, you took up the reins of management, and seemed to anticipate the fact that the house was eventually to be your own."

Miss Morton looked aghast. If one chose to think so, she looked as if detected in a false statement. Glancing round the room, she saw the eyes of Kitty French and of Marie, the maid, intently fixed on her. This seemed to unnerve her, and in a broken, trembling voice, almost a whine, she said:

"If I did so, it was only with a helpful motive. Mrs. Markham was so collapsed with the shock she had just sustained, that she was really incapable of giving orders. If I did so, it was only from a desire to be of service."

This seemed indeed plausible, and the most casual observer would know that Miss Morton's "helpfulness" could only be accomplished in a peremptory and dictatorial manner.

"Will you tell us why Miss Van Norman chose to leave you so large a bequest, when she had known you so slightly?" asked Mr. Benson.

Fessenden thought Miss Morton would resent this question, but instead she answered, willingly enough:

"Because she knew that except for my unfortunate quarrel with Richard Van Norman, many years ago, the place would have been mine any way."

"You mean you were to have married Mr. Van Norman."

"I mean just that."

Miss Morton looked a little defiant, but also an air of pride tinged her statement, and she seemed to be asserting her lifelong right to the property.

"Miss Van Norman, then, knew of your friendship with her uncle, and the reason of its cessation?"

"She learned of it about two years ago."

"How?"

"By finding some letters of mine among Mr. Van Norman's papers, shortly after his death."

"And in consequence of that discovery she willed you this house at her death?"

"Yes; that is, I suppose she must have done so—as she did so will it."

"But you did not know of it, and the reading of the will was to you a surprise?"

"Yes," declared Miss Morton, and though the coroner then dismissed her without comment on her statements, there were several present who did not believe the lady spoke veraciously.

Tom Willard was called next, and Fessenden wondered what

could be the testimony of a man who had not arrived on the scene until more than two hours after the deed was done.

And indeed there was little that Tom could say. Mr. Benson asked him to detail his own movements after he left the house the night before.

"There's little to tell," said Tom, "but I'll try to be exact. I went away from this house about ten o'clock, taking with me a suit-case full of clothes. I went directly to the Mapleton Inn, and though I don't know exactly, I should say I must have reached there in something less than ten minutes. Then I went to the office of the establishment, registered, and asked for a room. The proprietor gave me a good enough room, a bellboy picked up my bag, and I went to my room at once."

"And remained there?"

"Yes; later I rang for some ice water, which the same boy brought to me. Directly after that I turned in. I slept soundly until awakened by a knocking at my door at about two o'clock in the morning."

"The message from this house?"

"Yes. The landlord himself stood there when I opened the door, and told me I was wanted on the telephone. When I went to the telephone I heard Miss Morton's voice, and she asked me to come over here. I came as quickly as possible, and——"

Tom's voice broke at this point, and, feeling that his story was finished, Mr. Benson considerately asked him no further questions.

XI

"I DECLINE TO SAY"

Schuyler Carleton was questioned next When Mr. Benson asked him to tell his story, he hesitated and finally said that he would prefer to have the coroner ask direct questions, which he would answer.

"Did you go away from this house with the other guests at about ten o'clock last evening?"

"No, I was not here at dinner. I left at about half-past five in the afternoon."

"Where did you go?"

"I went directly home and remained there until late in the evening."

"Mr. Fessenden was with you?"

"He was with us at dinner. He is staying at my house, as he was invited to be best man at the wedding."

Though this statement came calmly from Carleton's lips, it was evident to all that he fully appreciated the tragic picture it suggested.

"He was with you through the evening?"

"Part of the time. He went early to his room, saying he had some business to attend to."

"Why were you two not here to dinner with Miss Van Norman?"

Fessenden looked up, surprised at this question. Surely Mr. Benson had gathered odd bits of information since morning.

Schuyler Carleton looked stern.

"I did not come because I did not wish to. Mr. Fessenden remained with me, saying he did not care to attend the dinner unless I did."

Carleton looked casually at Fessenden as he said this, and though there was no question in the glance, Rob nodded his head in corroboration of the witness.

"You spent the entire evening at home, then?"

"Yes, until a late hour."

"And then?"

"I returned here between eleven and twelve o'clock."

"To make a call?"

"No, I came upon an errand."

"What was the errand?"

"As it has no bearing upon the case, I think it is my privilege to decline to answer."

"You entered the house with a latch-key."

"I did."

"Is that latch-key your own property?"

"For the time, yes. Mrs. Markham gave it to me a few days ago, for my convenience, because I have occasion to come to the house so frequently."

"Was it your intention when you went away in the afternoon to return later?"

"It was."

"Upon this secret errand?"

"Yes."

"Did you expect to see Miss Van Norman when you entered the house with the latch-key?"

"I did not."

"And when you entered you discovered the tragedy in the library?"

Schuyler Carleton hesitated. His dry lips quivered and his whole frame shook with intense emotion. "Y-yes," he stammered.

But the mere fact of that hesitation instantly kindled a spark of suspicion in the minds of some of his hearers. Until that moment Carleton's excessive agitation had been attributed entirely to his grief at the awful fate which had come to his fiancée; but now, all at once, the man's demeanor gave an impression of something else.

Could it be guilt?

Fessenden looked at his friend curiously. In his mind, however, no slightest suspicion was aroused, but he wondered what it was that Carleton was keeping back. Surely the man must know that to make any mystery about his call at the Van Norman mansion the night before, was to invite immediate and justifiable suspicion.

The court had instructed the district attorney to be present at the inquest, and though that unobtrusive gentleman had taken notes, and otherwise shown a quiet interest in the proceedings, he now awakened to a more alert manner, and leaned forward to get a better look at the white, set face of the witness.

Carleton looked like a marble image. His refined, patrician features seemed even handsomer for their haggard agony. Surely he was in no way responsible for the awful deed that had been done, and yet just as surely he was possessed of some awful secret fear which kept every nerve strained and tense.

Endeavoring not to exhibit the surprise and dismay which he felt, Coroner Benson continued his questions.

69

"And then, when you discovered Miss Van Norman, what did you do?"

Carleton passed his hand across his white brow. "I hardly know," he said. "I was stunned—dazed. I went toward her, and, seeing the dagger on the floor, I picked it up mechanically, scarcely knowing what I did. I felt intuitively that the girl was dead, but I did not touch her, and, not knowing what else to do, I cried out for help."

"And turned on the lights?"

"I pushed several electric buttons, not knowing which were lights and which bells; my principal idea was to arouse the inmates of the house at once."

"Who first appeared in answer to your call?"

"Miss Dupuy came running downstairs at once, followed by Miss Van Norman's maid."

"And then you pointed to the paper that lay on the table near Miss Van Norman's hand."

"Yes; I could not speak, and I thought that would tell Miss Dupuy that Miss Van Norman had taken her own life."

"You thought, then, that Miss Van Norman wrote the message?"

"I thought so then—and I think so now."

This, of course, produced a sensation, but it was only evidenced by a deeper silence on the part of the startled audience.

"But Miss Dupuy asserts that she wrote it," said the coroner.

To this Schuyler Carleton merely gave a slight bow of his handsome head, but it said as plainly as words that his belief was not altered by Miss Dupuy's assertion.

"Granting for the moment, then," went on Mr. Benson, "that Miss Van Norman did write it, is the message intelligible to you?"

"Intelligible, yes;" said Carleton, "but, as I have said before, inexplicable."

This ambiguous speech meant little to most of the listeners, but it seemed to give Robert Fessenden food for thought, and he looked at Carleton with a new wonder in his eyes.

"Mr. Carleton," said the coroner, with a note of gravity in his voice, "I think it my duty to tell you that your own interests require you to state the nature of your errand to this house last night."

"I decline to do so."

"Then, will you state as exactly as you can the hour at which you entered the front door?"

"I don't know precisely. But Miss Dupuy has testified that she came downstairs in response to my call at half-past eleven. I came into the house a—a few moments before."

"That is all," said the coroner abruptly. "Mr. Hunt, if you please."

The man from headquarters, who had guarded the present room through the night, came in from the doorway where he had been standing.

"Will you tell what you know concerning Mr. Carleton's entrance last night?" said the coroner, briefly.

"I was on guard in the present room from nine o'clock on," said Mr. Hunt. "Of course I was on the watch-out for anything unusual, and alert to hear any sound. I heard the company go away at ten o'clock, I heard most of the people in the house go to their rooms right after that. I heard and I also saw Miss Dupuy go down to the library after that, and return to her room about half-past ten. I noticed all these things because that is my business, but they made no special impression on me, as they were but the natural proceedings of the people who belonged here. Of course I was only on the lookout for intruders. I heard the sound of a latch-key and I heard the front door open at exactly quarter after eleven. I stepped out into the hall, and, looking downstairs, I saw Mr. Carleton enter. I also saw Miss Dupuy in the upper hall looking over the banister. She, too, must have seen Mr. Carleton. But as all of this was none of my business, and as nobody had entered who hadn't a right to, I simply returned to my post. At half-past eleven I heard Mr. Carleton's cry, and saw the lights go up all over the house. Anything more, sir?"

"Not at present, Mr. Hunt. Miss Dupuy, did you hear Mr. Carleton come in?"

Cicely Dupuy turned an angry face toward Mr. Hunt and fairly glared at the mild-mannered man. She waited a moment before answering the coroner's question, and then as if with a sudden resolve she spoke a sharp, quick "Yes."

"And that was at quarter after eleven?"

"It was later," declared Cicely. "For Mr. Carleton told you himself that he went directly into the library as soon as he came into the house, and as I heard his cry at half-past eleven he must have entered only a few moments before."

Schuyler Carleton stared at Cicely, and she returned his gaze.

His face was absolutely inscrutable, a pallid mask, that might have concealed emotion of any sort. But there was a suggestion of fear in the strange eyes, as they gazed at Cicely, and though it was quickly suppressed it had been noted by those most interested.

The girl looked straight at him, with determination written in every line of her face. It was quite evident to the onlookers that a mental message was passing between these two.

71

"You are sure, Mr. Hunt, that your statement as to the time is correct?" said the coroner, turning again to him.

"Perfectly sure, sir. It is my business to be sure of the time."

"Mr. Carleton," said Mr. Benson, "there is an apparent discrepancy here, which it is advisable for you to explain. If you came into this house at quarter after eleven, and rang the bells for help at half-past eleven, what were you doing in the meantime?"

It was out at last. The coroner's question, though quietly put, was equivalent to an accusation. Every eye in the room was turned toward Carleton, and every ear waited in suspense for his reply.

At last the answer came. The dazed, uncertain look had returned to Carleton's face and his voice sounded mechanical, like that of an automaton, as he replied, "I decline to say."

"I think, Mr. Carleton, you can scarcely realize the gravity of the moment, or the mistake you are making in refusing to answer this question."

"I have nothing to say," repeated Carleton, and his pallor changed to a faint, angry flush of red.

"I am sorry," said Mr. Benson gently. He seemed to have lost his pompous manner in his genuine anxiety for his witness, and he looked sorrowfully at Carleton's impassive, yet stubborn face.

"As so much hinges on the question of who wrote that paper," he resumed, "I will make a test now that ought to convince us all. Miss Dupuy, you say that you wrote it, I believe."

"I did, yes, sir," said Cicely, stammering a little now, though she had been calm enough a few minutes before.

"Then you know the words on the paper,—by rote?"

"Yes, sir," said Cicely, uncertain of where this was leading.

"I will ask you, then, to take this paper and pencil, your own pencil and write the same words in the same way once more."

"Oh, don't ask me to do that!" implored Cicely, clasping her hands and looking very distressed.

"I not only ask you, but I direct you to do it, and do it at once."

An attendant handed pencil and paper to Cicely, and, after a glance at Carleton, who did not meet it, she began to write.

Though evidently agitated, she wrote clearly and evenly, and the paper she handed to Coroner Benson a moment later was practically an exact duplicate of the one found on the library table.

"It does not require a handwriting expert," said the coroner, "to declare that these two papers were written by the same hand. The penmanship is indeed similar to Miss Van Norman's, of whose writing I have here many specimens, but it is only similar. It is by no means identical. You may all examine these at your leisure and can only agree to what I say."

The district attorney, who had been comparing the papers, laid them down with an air of finality that proved his agreement with the statements made.

"And so," went on Mr. Benson, "granting, as we must, that Miss Dupuy wrote the paper, we have nothing whatever to indicate that this case is a suicide. We are, therefore, seeking a murderer, and our most earnest efforts must be made to that end. I trust, Mr. Carleton, now that you can no longer think Miss Van Norman wrote the message, that you will aid us in our work by stating frankly how you were occupied during that quarter-hour which elapsed between your entering the house and your raising the alarm?"

But Carleton preserved his stony calm.

"There was no quarter-hour," he said; "I may have stepped into the drawing-room a moment before going to the library, but I gave the alarm almost immediately on entering the house. Certainly immediately on my discovery of—of the scene in the library."

Cicely looked defiantly at Mr. Hunt, who, in his turn, looked perplexed. The man had no wish to insinuate anything against Mr. Carleton, but as he had said, it was his business to know the time, and he knew that Mr. Carleton came into the house at quarter after eleven, and not at half-past.

The pause that followed was broken by Coroner Benson's voice. "There is nothing more to be done at present. The inquest is adjourned until to-morrow afternoon. But we have discovered that there has been a crime committed. There is no doubt that Miss Van Norman was murdered, and that the crime took place between half-past ten and half-past eleven last night. It is our duty to spare no effort to discover the criminal. As an audience you are now dismissed."

XII

DOROTHY BURT

The people rose slowly from their chairs, and most of them looked as if they did not quite comprehend what it all meant. Among these was Carleton himself. He seemed oblivious to the fact that he was—at least tacitly—an accused man, and stood quietly, as if awaiting any further developments that might come.

"Look at Schuyler," said Kitty French to Fessenden. The two had withdrawn to a quiet corner to discuss the affair. But Kitty was doing most of the talking, while Fessenden was quiet and seemed preoccupied. "Of course I suppose he must have killed Madeleine," went on Kitty, "but it's so hard to believe it, after all. I've tried to think of a reason for it, and this is the only one I can think of. They quarrelled yesterday afternoon, and he went away in a huff. I believe he came back last night to make it up with her, and then they quarrelled again and he stabbed her."

Fessenden looked at her thoughtfully. "I think that Hunt man testified accurately," he said. "And if so, Carleton was in the house just fifteen minutes before he gave the alarm. Now, fifteen minutes is an awfully short time to quarrel with anybody so desperately that it leads to a murder."

"That's true; but they both have very quick tempers. At least Madeleine had. She didn't often do it, but when she did fly into a fury it was as quick as a flash. I've never seen Mr. Carleton angry, but I know he can be, for Maddy told me so."

"Still, a quarter of an hour is too short a time for a fatal quarrel, I think. If Carleton killed her he came here for that purpose, and it was done premeditatedly."

"Why do you say 'if he killed her'? It's been proved she didn't kill herself; it's been proved that no one could enter the house without a latch-key, and it's been proved that the deed was done in that one hour between half-past ten and half-past eleven. So it had to be Mr. Carleton."

"Miss French, you have a logical mind, and I think you'd make a clever little detective. But you have overlooked the possibility that she was killed by some one in the house."

"Some of us?" Kitty's look of amazement almost made Fessenden smile.

"Not you or Miss Gardner," he said. "But a burglar might have been concealed in the house."

74

"I never thought of that!" exclaimed Kitty, her eyes opening wide at the thought. "Why, he might have killed us all!"

"It isn't a very plausible theory," said Fessenden, unheeding the girl's remark, "and yet I could think of nothing else. Every instinct of my mind denies Carleton's guilt. Why, he isn't that sort of a man!"

"Perhaps he isn't as good as he looks," said Kitty, wagging her head wisely. "I know a lot about him. You know he wasn't a bit in love with Maddy."

"You hinted that before. And was he really a mere fortune-hunter? I can't believe that of Carleton. I've known the man for years."

"He must have been, or else why did he marry her? He's in love with another girl."

"He is! Who?"

"I don't know who. But Madeleine hinted it to me only a few days ago. It made her miserable. And that's why everybody thought she wrote that paper that said, 'I love S., but he does not love me.'"

"And you don't know who this rival is?"

"No, but I know what she's like. She's the 'clinging rosebud' effect."

"What do you mean?"

"Just that. You know Madeleine was a big, grand, splendid type,—majestic and haughty; and she thought Schuyler loved better some little, timid girl, who would sort of look up to him, and need his protection."

Fessenden looked steadily at Miss French. "Are you imagining all this," he said, "or is it true?"

"Both," responded Kitty, with a charming little smile. "Maddy just hinted it to me, and I guessed the rest. You know, I have detective instinct too, as well as you."

"You have, indeed;" and Rob gave an admiring glance to the pouting red lips, and roguish eyes. "But tell me more about it."

"There isn't much to tell," said Kitty, looking thoughtful, "but there's a lot to deduce."

"Well, tell me what there is to tell, and then we'll both deduce."

It pleased Kitty greatly to imagine she was really helping Fessenden, and she went glibly on:

"Why, you see, Maddy was unhappy,—we all know that,—and it was for some reason connected with Schuyler. Yet they were to be married, all the same. But sometimes Maddy has asked me, with such a wistful look, if I didn't think men preferred little, kittenish girls to big, proud ones like herself."

"And you, being a little, kittenish girl, said yes?"

"Don't be rude," said Kitty, flashing a smile at him. "I am kittenish in name only. And I am not little!"

"You are, compared to Miss Van Norman's type."

"Oh, yes; she was like a beautiful Amazon. Well, she either had reason to think, or she imagined, that Schuyler pretended to love her, and was really in love with some dear little clinging rosebud."

"Clinging rosebud! What an absurd expression! And yet—by Jove!—it just fits her! And Miss Van Norman said to me—oh, I say, Miss French, don't you know who the rosebud is?"

"No," said Kitty, wondering at his sudden look of dismay.

"Well, I do! Oh, this is getting dreadful. Come outside with me and let's look into this idea. I hope it's only an idea!"

Throwing a soft fawn-colored cape round her, and drawing its pink-lined hood over her curly hair, Kitty went with Fessenden out on the lawn and down to the little arbor where they had sat before.

"Did you ever hear of Dorothy Burt?" he asked, almost in a whisper.

"No; who is she?"

"Well, she's your 'clinging rosebud,' I'm sure of it! And I'll tell you why."

"First tell me who she is."

"She's Mrs. Carleton's companion. Schuyler's mother, you know. She lives in the Carleton household, and she is the sweetest, prettiest, shyest little thing you ever saw! 'Clinging rosebud' just fits her."

"Indeed!" said Kitty, who had suddenly lost interest in the conversation. And indeed, few girls of Kitty's disposition would have enjoyed this enthusiastic eulogy of another.

"I don't admire that sort, myself," went on Rob, who was tactfully observant; "I like a little more spirit and vivacity." Kitty beamed once more. "But she's a wonder, of her own class. I was there at dinner last night, you know, and I saw her for the first time. And, though I thought nothing of it at the time, I can look back now and see that she adores Schuyler. Why, she scarcely took her eyes off him at dinner, and she ate next to nothing. Poor little girl, I believe she was awfully cut up at his approaching marriage."

"And what was Schuyler's attitude toward her?" Kitty was interested enough now.

Fessenden looked very grave and was silent for a time.

"It's a beastly thing to say," he observed at last, "but if Schuyler had been in love with that girl, and wanted to conceal the fact, he couldn't have acted differently from the way he did act."

"Was he kind to her?"

"Yes, kind, but with a restrained air, as if he felt it his duty to show indifference toward her."

"Was she with you after dinner?"

Fessenden thought.

"I went to my room early; and Mrs. Carleton had then already excused herself. Yes,—I left Schuyler and Miss Burt in the drawing-room, and later I saw them from my window, strolling through the rose-garden."

"On his wedding eve!" exclaimed Kitty, with a look akin to horror in her eyes.

"Yes; and I thought nothing of it, for I simply assumed that he was devoted to Miss Van Norman, and was merely pleasant to his mother's companion. But—in view of something Miss Van Norman said to me yesterday—can it be it was only yesterday?—the matter becomes serious."

"What did she say?"

"It seems like betraying a confidence, and yet it isn't, for we must discover if it means anything. But she said to me, with real agitation, 'Do you know Dorothy Burt?' At that time, I hadn't met Miss Burt, and had never heard of her, so I said: 'No; who is she?' 'Nobody,' said Miss Van Norman, 'less than nobody! Never mention her to me again!' Her voice, even more than her words, betokened grief and even anger, so of course the subject was dropped. But doesn't that prove her anxious about the girl, if not really jealous?"

"Of course it does," said Kitty. "I know that's the one that has been troubling Madeleine. Oh, how dreadful it all is!"

"And then, too," Fessenden said, still reminiscently, "Miss Van Norman said she wanted to go away from Mapleton immediately after her wedding, and never return here again."

"Did she say that! Then, of course, it was only so that Schuyler should never see the Burt girl again. Poor, dear Maddy; she was so proud, and so self-contained. But how she must have suffered! You see, she knew Schuyler admired her, and respected her and all that, and she must have thought that, once removed from the presence of the rosebud girl, he would forget her."

"But I can't understand old Schuyler marrying Miss Van Norman if he didn't truly love her. You know, Miss French, that man and I have been stanch friends for years; and though I rarely see him, I know his honorable nature, and I can't believe he would marry one woman while loving another."

"He didn't," said Kitty in a meaning voice that expressed far more than the words signified.

Fessenden drew back in horror.

77

"Don't!" he cried. "You can't mean that Schuyler put Miss Van Norman out of the way to clear the path for Miss Burt!"

"I don't mean anything," said Kitty, rather contradictorily. "But, as I said, Maddy was not killed by any one inside the house—I'm sure of that—and no one from outside could get in, except Schuyler—and he had a motive. Don't you always, in detective work, look for the motive?"

"Yes, but this is too horrible!"

"All murders are 'too horrible.' But I tell you it must have been Schuyler—it couldn't have been Miss Burt!"

"Don't be absurd! That little girl couldn't kill a fly, I'm sure. I wish you could see her, Miss French. Then you'd understand how her very contrast to Miss Van Norman's splendid beauty would fascinate Schuyler. And I know he was fascinated. I saw it in his repressed manner last evening, though I didn't realize it then as I do now."

"I have a theory," said Kitty slowly. "You know Mr. Carleton went away yesterday afternoon rather angry at Maddy. She had carried her flirtation with Tom a little too far, and Mr. Carleton resented it. I don't blame him,—the very day before the wedding,—but it was partly his fault, too. Well, suppose he went home, rather upset over the quarrel, and then seeing Miss Burt, and her probably mild, angelic ways (I'm sure she has them!)—suppose he wished he could be off with Maddy, and marry Miss Burt instead."

"But he wouldn't kill his fiancée, if he did think that!"

"Wait a minute. Then suppose, after the evening in the rose-garden with the gentle, clinging little girl, he concluded he never could be happy with Maddy, and suppose he came at eleven o'clock, or whatever time it was, to tell her so, and to ask her to set him free."

"On the eve of the wedding day? With the house already in gala dress for the ceremony?"

"Yes, suppose the very nearness of the ceremony made it seem to him impossible to go through with it."

"Well?"

"Well, and then suppose he did ask Madeleine to free him, and suppose she refused. And she would refuse! I know her nature well enough to know she never would give him up to the other girl if she could help it. And then suppose, when she refused to free him,—you know he has a fearfully quick temper, and that awful paper-cutter lay right there, handy,—suppose he stabbed her in a moment of desperate anger."

"I can't think it," said Rob, after a pause; "I've tried, and I can't. But, suppose all you say is true as far as this; suppose he asked her to free him, because he loved another, and suppose she was so grieved and mortified at this, that in her own sudden fit of angry jealousy,—you know she had a quick temper, also,—suppose she picked up the dagger and turned it upon herself, as she had sometimes said she would do."

Kitty listened attentively. "It might be so," she said slowly; "you may be nearer the truth than I. But I do believe that one of us must be right. Of course, this leaves the written paper out of the question entirely."

"That written paper hasn't been thoroughly explained yet," exclaimed the young man. "Now, look here, Miss French, I'm not going to wait to be officially employed on this case, though I am going to offer Carleton my legal services, but I mean to do a little investigating on my own account. The sooner inquiries are made, the more information is usually obtained. Can you arrange that I shall have an interview with Miss Dupuy?"

"I think I can," said Kitty; "but if you let it appear that you're inquisitive she won't tell you a thing. Suppose we just talk to her casually, you and I. I won't bother you."

"Indeed you won't. You'll be of first-class help. When can we see her?"

While they had been talking, other things had been happening in the drawing-room. The people who had been gathered there had all disappeared, and, under the active superintendence of Miss Morton, the florist's men who had put up the decorations were now taking them away. The whole room was in confusion, and Kitty and Mr. Fessenden were glad to escape to some more habitable place.

"Wait here," said Kitty, as they passed through the hall, "and I'll be back in a moment."

Kitty flew upstairs, and soon returned, saying that Miss Dupuy would be glad to talk with them both in Madeleine's sitting-room.

XIII

AN INTERVIEW WITH CICELY

This sitting-room was on the second floor, directly back of Madeleine's bedroom, the bedroom being above the library. Miss Dupuy's own room was back of this and communicated with it.

The sitting-room was a pleasant place, with large light windows and easy chairs and couches. A large and well-filled desk seemed to prove the necessity of a social secretary, if Miss Van Norman cared to have any leisure hours.

Surrounded by letters and papers, Cicely sat at the desk as they entered, but immediately rose to meet them.

Kitty's tact in requesting the interview had apparently been successful, for Miss Dupuy was gracious and affable.

But after some desultory conversation which amounted to nothing, Fessenden concluded a direct course would be better.

"Miss Dupuy," he said, "I'm a detective, at least in an amateur way."

Cicely gave a start and a look of fear came into her eyes.

"I have the interests of Schuyler Carleton at heart," the young man continued, "and my efforts shall be primarily directed toward clearing him from any breath of suspicion that may seem to have fallen upon him."

"O, thank you!" cried Cicely, clasping her hands and showing such genuine gratitude that Fessenden was startled by a new idea.

"I'm sure," he said, "that you'll give me any help in your power. As Miss Van Norman's private secretary, of course you know most of the details of her daily life."

"Yes; but I don't see why I should tell everything to that Benson man!"

"You should tell him only such things as may have a bearing on this mystery that we are trying to clear up."

"Then I know nothing to tell. I know nothing about the mystery."

"No, Cicely," said Kitty, in a soothing voice, "of course you know nothing definite; but if you could tell us some few things that may seem to you unimportant, we—that is, Mr. Fessenden—might find them of great help."

"Well," returned Cicely slowly, "you may ask questions, if you choose, Mr. Fessenden, and I will answer or not, as I prefer."

"Thank you, Miss Dupuy. You may feel sure I will ask only the

80

ones I consider necessary to the work I have undertaken. And first of all, was Miss Van Norman in love with Carleton?"

"She was indeed, desperately so."

"Yet she seemed greatly attached to her cousin, Mr. Willard."

"That was partly a cousinly affection, and partly a sort of coquetry to pique Mr. Carleton."

"And was Carleton devoted to her?"

"Must I answer that?" Cicely's eyes looked troubled.

"Yes, you must." Fessenden's voice was very gentle.

"Then he was not devoted to her; in fact, he loved another."

"Who is this other?"

"Dorothy Burt, his mother's companion, who lives at the Carleton home."

"Did Miss Van Norman know this?"

"Yes, she learned of it lately, and it broke her heart. That is why she was so uncertain and erratic in her moods; that is why she coquetted with Mr. Willard, to arouse Schuyler Carleton's jealousy."

"This throws a new light on it all," said Fessenden gravely. "And this Miss Burt—did she return Carleton's regard?"

"I don't know," said Cicely, and her agitation seemed to increase, though she tried hard to conceal it. "Of course Miss Van Norman didn't speak openly of this matter, but I knew her so well that I easily divined from her moods and her actions that she knew she had a rival in Mr. Carleton's affections."

"Then he cared more for her in time past?"

"Yes, until that girl came to live with his mother. She's a designing little thing, and she just twisted Mr. Carleton round her finger."

"Do you know her personally, Miss Dupuy?"

A look of intense hatred came over Cicely's expressive face.

"No! I wouldn't meet her for anything. But I have seen her, and I know perfectly well that Mr. Carleton cares for her more than he did for Miss Van Norman."

"Yet he was about to marry Miss Van Norman."

"Yes; because they were engaged before he saw the Burt girl. Then, you see, he didn't think it honorable to refuse to marry her, and she——"

"He had asked her, then, to give him back his freedom?"

"Yes, he had. And Miss Van Norman very rightly refused to do so."

"Oh, Cicely," cried Kitty, "do you know this, or are you only surmising it?"

"I know it, Miss French. In her sorrow over the matter, Miss Van Norman often confided in me as in a friend."

81

"And you were a good friend to her, I'm sure," said Fessenden heartily. "Now, Miss Dupuy, do you think it could have been possible that Mr. Carleton came here late last night to ask Miss Van Norman once again to release him from the marriage?"

"He might have done so," said Cicely in a noncommittal tone. "He was very much annoyed at her behavior with Mr. Willard in the afternoon."

"But that was on purpose to annoy him?"

"Yes, and it succeeded."

"How do you know all this?"

"Miss Van Norman intimated as much just before dinner, when we were here alone. She feared Mr. Carleton was so angry he wouldn't come to dinner at all."

"And he didn't."

"No, he didn't."

"But, Miss Dupuy, it would scarcely be possible to think that if he did return later to ask his release—it would not be possible to think that on Miss Van Norman's refusal to release him he—was so incensed against her that——"

"Oh, no, no!" cried Cicely. "Of course he didn't kill her! Of course he didn't! She killed herself! I don't care what any one says—I know she killed herself!"

"If so," said Fessenden, "we must prove it by keeping on with our investigations. And now, Miss Dupuy, will you tell me what was your errand when you returned to the library late last night, when the two doctors were alone there in charge of the room?"

"I didn't!" declared Cicely, her cheeks flaming and her blue eyes fairly glaring at her interrogator.

"Please stick to the truth, Miss Dupuy," said Fessenden coldly. "If you don't, we can't credit any of your statements. You opened the door very softly, and were about to enter, when you spied the doctors and withdrew."

"I went to get that paper," said Cicely, somewhat sulkily.

"Why did you want that?"

"Because it was mine. I had a right to it."

"Then why didn't you go on in and get it? The doctors' presence need have made no difference."

"I don't know why I didn't! I wish you'd stop asking questions!"

"I will, in a moment. You are sure you wrote that paper yourself?"

"Of course I am!" The answer was snapped out pertly.

"And you wrote it meaning yourself? You didn't write it with the intent that it should be taken for Miss Van Norman's message?"

Cicely eyes dropped involuntarily. Then she raised them, and

82

stared straight at Fessenden. "What do you mean?" she asked haughtily.

"Just what I say. Was that written paper an expression of your own heart's secret?"

It must have been because of Fessenden's magnetism, or compelling sympathy, but for some reason Cicely took no offense at this, and answered simply, "Yes."

"Strange," mused Rob, "how that man won so many women's hearts."

"No, it isn't strange," said Cicely, also in slow, thoughtful tones. And then, suddenly realizing the admission she had made, and seeing how she had revealed her own secret she flew into a rage.

"What do you mean?" she cried. "I didn't refer to Mr. Carleton."

"Yes, you did," said Fessenden, so quietly that again Cicely was silent, and Kitty sat surprised almost to breathlessness.

"There is to be only truth between us," went on Rob. "You did mean Mr. Carleton, by the letter 'S'; but have no fear, your secret shall be respected. Now we will have only the truth—remember that. So please tell me frankly at what time you saw Mr. Carleton come into the house last night?"

"Just a few moments before half-past eleven." Cicely said this glibly, as if reciting a carefully-conned lesson.

"Wait a moment—you forget that Mr. Hunt fixed the time at quarter after eleven, and that he saw you looking over the baluster at the same time."

With an agonized cry of dismay, Miss Dupuy fainted into utter unconsciousness.

Perplexed and baffled in his inquiries, Fessenden saw that for the moment Miss Dupuy's physical condition was of paramount importance, and at Kitty's request he rang for Marie. Even before she came the others had placed Cicely gently on a couch, and when the maid arrived Fessenden left the room, knowing that the girl was properly cared for.

Going downstairs again, he was about to make his adieux to Mrs. Markham and leave the house, when Kitty French, coming down soon after him, asked him to stay a few minutes longer.

The sight of her pretty face drove more serious thoughts from his mind, and he turned, more than willing to follow where she led. "Oh, whistle, and I'll come to you," he whispered. But Kitty had weighty information to impart, and was in no mood for trifling. They found a quiet corner, and then Kitty told him that Cicely had regained consciousness almost immediately, but that just before she did so, she cried out sharply, "They must not think Schuyler did it! They must not!"

"And so," said Kitty, astutely, "you see, it's as I told you. Mr. Carleton did kill Maddy, and Cicely knows it, but she doesn't want other people to find it out, because she's in love with him herself!"

Rob Fessenden gave his companion an admiring glance.

"That's good reasoning and sound logic," he said; "and I'd subscribe to it if it were anybody but old Schuyler. But I can't and won't believe that man guilty without further evidence than that of a fainting, hysterical woman."

"Everybody seems to be in love with Mr. Carleton," said Kitty, demurely.

"You're not, are you?" said Rob, so quickly that Kitty blushed.

"No, I'm not," she declared. "He's a stunning-looking man, and that superior, impassive way of his catches some women, but I don't care for it. I prefer a more enthusiastic temperament."

"Like mine," said Rob casually.

"Have you a temperament?" said Kitty saucily. "It isn't at all noticeable."

"It will be, after you know me better. But Miss French, since you've raised this question of Miss Dupuy's evidence, let me tell you what it means to me. Or, rather, what it seems to point to, for it's all too vague for us to draw any real conclusions. But, as a first impression, my suspicion turns toward Miss Dupuy herself rather than Carleton."

"Cicely! You don't mean she killed Maddy! Oh, how can you?"

"Now, don't fly into hysterics yourself. Wait a minute. I haven't accused her at all. But look at it. Miss Van Norman was certainly killed by Carleton, or by some one already in the house. It has been proved that nobody outside could get in. Now if the criminal is some one in the house, we must consider each one in turn. And if by chance we consider Miss Dupuy first, we must admit a motive."

"What motive?"

"Why, that of a jealous woman. Miss Van Norman was just about to marry the man Miss Dupuy is in love with. Perhaps—do have patience, I'm merely supposing—perhaps she has vainly urged Miss Van Norman to give him up, and, finding she wouldn't do so, at the last minute she prevented the marriage herself,—putting that paper on the table to make it appear a suicide. This would explain her stealthy attempt to regain possession of the paper later."

"Why should she want it?"

"So that it couldn't be proved not to be in Miss Van Norman's writing."

"It's ingenious on your part," said Kitty slowly, "but it can't be true. Cicely may be in love with Schuyler, but she wouldn't kill Maddy because of that."

"Who can tell what a hysterical, jealous woman will do?" said Rob, with the air of an oracle. "And moreover, to my mind, that explains her half-conscious exclamation of which you just told me. When she said, 'They must not think Schuyler did it,' it meant that she knew he didn't do it, but she didn't want suspicion to rest on him. That's why she insists it was a suicide."

So in earnest was Fessenden that Kitty felt almost convinced there was something in his theory.

"But it can't be," she said, at last, with an air of finality. "It wouldn't be possible for Cicely to do such a thing! I know her too well!"

"Then, Miss French, if that, to you, is a logical argument, you must admit mine. It wouldn't be possible for Carleton to do such a thing! I know him too well!"

Kitty had to smile at the imitation of the strong inflections she had used, and, too, she had to admit that one opinion was as permissible as the other.

"You see," went on Rob quietly, "we're not really assuming Miss Dupuy's guilt, we're only seeing where these deductions lead us. Suppose, for the moment, that Miss Dupuy did, during that half-hour in the library, have an altercation with Miss Van Norman, and just suppose,—or imagine, if you prefer the word,—that she turned the dagger upon her friend and employer, wouldn't her subsequent acts have been just as they were? At Mr. Carleton's alarm, she came downstairs, fully dressed; later she tried to remove secretly that written paper; always at serious questioning she faints or flies into hysterics; and, naturally, when suspicion comes near the man she cares for, she tries to turn it off. And then, too, Miss French, a very strong point against her is that she was the last one, so far as we know, to see Miss Van Norman alive. Of course, the murderer was the last one; but I mean, of the witnesses, Miss Dupuy was the latest known to be with Miss Van Norman. Thus, her evidence cannot be corroborated, and it may or may not be true. If she is the guilty one, we cannot expect the truth from her, and so we must at least admit that there is room for investigation, if not suspicion."

"I suppose you are right," said Kitty slowly; "a man's mind is said to be more logical. A woman depends more on her intuition. Now, my intuition tells me that Cicely Dupuy can not be the guilty one."

"At risk of tiresome repetition," returned Fessenden, "I must say again that that is no more convincing than my 'intuition' that Carleton can not be the guilty one."

Kitty's smile showed her quick appreciation of this point, and Rob went on:

"Though suspicion, so far, is cast in no other direction, it is only fair to consider all the others in the house. This will, of course, be done in due time. I approve of Mr. Benson, and I think, though his manners are pompous and at times egotistical, he has a good mind and a quick intelligence. He will do his part, I am sure, and then, if necessary, others will be brought into the case. But, as Carleton's friend, I shall devote all my energies to clearing him from what I know is an unjust suspicion."

And then Rob Fessenden went away. Mrs. Markham asked him to remain to dinner, but he declined, preferring to go home with Carleton. He said he would return next morning, and said too that he meant to stay in Mapleton as long as he could be of any service to any of his friends.

This decision was, of course, the result of his great friendship for Carleton, and his general interest in the Van Norman case, but it was also partly brought about by the bewitching personality of Kitty French and the impression she had made on his not usually susceptible heart.

And being master of his own time, Fessenden resolved to stay for a few days and observe developments along several lines.

XIV

THE CARLETON HOUSEHOLD

Mrs. Carleton's dinner table that evening presented a very different atmosphere from the night before.

The hostess herself was present only by a strong effort of will power. Mrs. Carleton had been greatly overcome by the shock of the dreadful news, and, aside from the sadness and horror of the tragedy, she was exceedingly disappointed at what seemed to her the ruin of her son's future.

The Carletons were an old and aristocratic family, though by no means possessed of great fortune.

The alliance, therefore, with the wealth of the Van Norman estate, and the power of the Van Norman name, seemed to Mrs. Carleton the crowning glory of her son's career, and she had been devoutly thankful when the wedding-day was set.

Though stubbornly unwilling to believe it, she had of late been forced to notice the growing attachment between Schuyler and her own companion, Miss Burt, and had it not been for the surety of the approaching wedding, she would have dismissed the girl. But so certain was she that her son's ambitions, like her own, were centred on the Van Norman name, she could not believe that Schuyler would let himself become greatly interested in Dorothy Burt.

But she did not allow for that mischievous Imp of Romance who plays havoc with hearts without saying "by your leave."

And partly because of her own dainty charm, partly because of her contrast to Madeleine's magnificence, Dorothy Burt crept into Schuyler Carleton's affections before either of them realized it, and when they did discover the surprising fact, it did not seem to dismay them as it should have done.

But it troubled them; for Schuyler well knew that honor, expediency, and good judgment all held him bound to Miss Van Norman, and Dorothy Burt knew it equally well.

And, whether or not with an ulterior motive, she had made no claim on him from the first. She had admitted her love for him, but in the same breath had avowed her appreciation of its hopelessness. Even if he hinted at a possible transfer of his allegiance, she had hushed him at once, saying it was impossible for him to do otherwise than to be true to his troth, and that he must forget her, as she should—try to—forget him.

This nobility on her part only made Carleton love her more, and though continuing to admire his beautiful fiancée, his real affection was all for little Dorothy.

She came to dinner that night, soft and lovely in a simple white frock, her pathetic eyes wide open in grief and sorrow, her rosebud mouth drooping and tremulous at the corners.

Fessenden watched her. Without appearing to do so, he noted every expression that flitted across her baby face.

And he was greatly disturbed.

The night before he had paid slight attention to her. To be sure, Miss Van Norman had spoken her name in the afternoon, but it had meant little to him, and, thinking of her merely as Mrs. Carleton's companion, or secretary, he wasn't sure which, he had been conventionally polite and no more. But to-night she was a factor in the case, and must be reckoned with.

As Fessenden watched her, he saw, with a growing conviction, as sure as it was awful, that she was relieved at Miss Van Norman's death.

Gentle, tender little girl as she seemed, it was nevertheless true that the removal of the obstacle between Carleton and herself gave her only joy. She tried to hide this. She cleverly simulated grief, horror, surprise, interest,—all the emotions called forth by the conversation, which unavoidably pursued only one course. In fact, Miss Burt took her cue every time from Mrs. Carleton, and expressed opinions that invariably coincided with hers.

It began to dawn upon Fessenden that the girl was unusually clever, the more so, he thought, that she was consciously concealing her cleverness by a cloak of demure innocence, and careful unostentation. Never did she put herself forward; never did she show undue interest in Schuyler, personally.

Fessenden reasoned that the game being now in her own hands, she could afford to stand back and await developments.

Then came the next thought: how came the game so fortuitously into her own hands? Was it, even indirectly, due to her own instigation?

"Pshaw!" he thought to himself. "I'm growing absurdly suspicious. I won't believe wrong of that girl until I have some scrap of a hint to base it on."

And yet he knew in his own heart if Dorothy Burt had wanted to connive in the slightest degree in the removal of her rival, she was quite capable of doing so, notwithstanding her very evident effect of pretty helplessness.

"When an excessively clever young woman assumes an utterly inefficient air," he thought, "it must be for some undeclared purpose;" and he felt an absurd thrill of satisfaction that though

88

Kitty French was undeniably clever, she put on no ingénue arts to hide it.

Then Kitty's phrase of "a clinging rosebud" came to his mind, and he realized its exceeding aptness to describe Dorothy Burt. Her appealing eyes and wistful, curved mouth were enough to lure a man who loved her to almost any deed of daring.

"Even murder?" flashed into his brain, and he recoiled at the thought. Old Schuyler might have been made to forget his fealty; he might have been unable to steel his heart against those subtle charms; he might have thrown to the winds his honor and his faith; but surely, never, never, could he have committed that dreadful deed, even for love of this angel-faced siren.

"Could she?"

The words fairly burned into Fessenden's brain. The sudden thought set his mind whirling. Could she? Why, no, of course not! Absurd! Yes, but could she? What? That child? That baby-girl? Those tiny, rose-leaf hands! Yes, but could she?

"No!" said Fessenden angrily, and then realized that he had spoken aloud, and his hearers were looking at him with indulgent curiosity.

"Forgive me," he said, smiling as he looked at Mrs. Carleton. "My fancy took a short but distant flight, and I had to speak to it sternly by way of reproof."

"I didn't know a lawyer could be fanciful," said Mrs. Carleton. "I thought that privilege was reserved for poets."

"Thank you for a pretty compliment to our profession," said Rob. "We lawyers are too often accused of giving rein to our fancy, when we should be strapped to the saddle of slow but sure Truth."

"But can you arrive anywhere on such a prosaic steed?" asked Miss Burt, smiling at his words.

"Yes," said Rob; "we can arrive at facts."

What prompted him to speak so curtly, he didn't know; but his speech did not at all please Miss Burt. Her color flew to her cheeks, though she said nothing, and then, as Mrs. Carleton rose from the table, the two ladies smiled and withdrew, leaving Rob alone with his host.

"It's all right, old boy, of course," said Carleton, "but did you have any reason for flouting poor little Dorothy like that?"

"No, I didn't," said Fessenden honestly and apologetically. "I spoke without thinking, and I'm sorry for it."

"All right—it's nothing. Now, Rob, old fellow, you can't deceive me. I saw a curious expression in your eyes as you looked at Miss Burt to-night, and—well, there is no need of words between us, so I'll only tell you you're all wrong there. You look for hidden meanings and veiled allusions in everything that girl says, and there aren't any. She's as frank and open-natured as she can be, and—forgive me—but I want you to let her alone."

Fessenden was astounded. First, at Carleton's insight in discovering his thoughts, and second, at Carleton's mistaken judgment of Miss Burt's nature.

But he only said, "All right, Schuyler; what you say, goes. Would you rather not talk at all about the Van Norman affair?" Fessenden spoke thus casually, for he felt sure it would make it easier for Carleton than if he betrayed a deeper interest.

"Oh, I don't care. You know, of course, how deeply it affects me and my whole life. I know your sympathy and good-fellowship. There's not much more to say, is there?"

"Why, yes, Carleton; there is. As your friend, and also in the interests of justice, I am more than anxious to discover the villain who did the horrid deed, and though the inquest people are doing all they can, I want to add my efforts to theirs, in hope of helping them,—and you."

"Don't bother about me, Rob. I don't care if they never discover the culprit. Miss Van Norman is gone; it can't restore her to life if they do learn who killed her."

Fessenden looked mystified.

"That's strange talk, Schuyler,—but of course you're fearfully upset, and I suppose just at first it isn't surprising that you feel that way. But surely,—as man to man, now,—you want to find and punish the wretch that put an end to that beautiful young life."

"Yes,—I suppose so;" Carleton spoke hesitatingly, and drew his hand across his brow in the same dazed way he did when in the witness box.

"You're done up, old man, and I'm not going to bother you to-night. But I'm on the hunt, if you aren't, and I'm going ahead on a few little trails, hoping they'll lead to something of more importance. By the way, what were you doing in those few minutes last night between your entering the house and entering the library?"

Carleton stared at his guest.

"I don't know what you mean," he said.

"Yes, you do. You went in at eleven-fifteen, and you called for help at eleven-thirty."

"No,—it didn't take as long as that." Carleton's eyes had a far-away look, and Rob grasped his arm and shook him, as he said:

"Drop it, man! Drop that half-dazed way of speaking! Tell me, clearly, what did you do in that short interval?"

"I refuse to state," said Carleton quietly, but with a direct glance now that made Fessenden cease his insistence.

"Very well," he said; "it's of no consequence. Now tell me what you were doing last evening before you went over to the house?"

At this Carleton showed a disposition to be both haughty and ironical.

"Am I being questioned," he said, "and by you? Well, before I went to Miss Van Norman's I was walking in the rose-garden with Miss Burt. You saw me from your window."

"I did," said Rob gravely. "Were you with Miss Burt until the time of your going over to the Van Norman house?"

"No," said Carleton, with sarcastic intonation. "I said good-night to Miss Burt about three-quarters of an hour before I started to go over to Miss Van Norman's. Do you want to know what I did during that interval?"

"Yes."

"I was in my own room—my den. I did what many a man does on the eve of his wedding. I burned up a few notes,—perhaps a photograph or two,—and one withered rose-bud,—a 'keepsake.' Does this interest you?"

"Not especially, but, Schuyler, do drop that resentful air. I'm not quizzing you, and if you don't want to talk about the subject at all, we won't."

"Very well,—I don't."

"Very well, then."

The two men rose, and as Carleton held out his hand Rob grasped it and shook it heartily, then they went to the drawing-room and rejoined the ladies.

The Van Norman affair was not mentioned again that evening.

All felt a certain oppression in the atmosphere, and all tried to dispel it, but it was not easy. Uninteresting topics of conversation were tossed from one to another, but each felt relieved when at last Mrs. Carleton rose to go upstairs and the evening was at an end.

Fessenden went to his room, his brain a whirlwind of conflicting thoughts.

He sat down by an open window and endeavored to classify them into some sort of order.

First, he was annoyed at Carleton's inexplicable attitude. Granting he was in love with Miss Burt, he had no reason to act so unconcerned about the Van Norman tragedy. And yet Schuyler's was a peculiar nature, and doubtless all this strange behavior of his was merely the effort to hide his real sorrow.

But again, if he were in love with Miss Burt, his sorrow for the loss of Madeleine was for the loss of her fortune and not herself.

91

This Fessenden refused to believe, but the more he refused to believe it, the more it came back to him. Then there was his new notion, that came to him at dinner, about Miss Burt. Carleton said she was the ingenuous, timid girl she looked, but Rob couldn't believe it. Executive ability showed in that determined little chin. Veiled cunning lurked in the shadows of those innocent eyes. And the girl had a motive. Surely she wanted her rival out of her way. Then she had said good-night to Schuyler nearly an hour before he went over to Madeleine's. Could she have—but, nonsense! Even if she had been so inclined, how could she have entered the house? Ah, that settled it! She couldn't. And Fessenden was honestly glad of it. Honestly glad that he had proved to himself that Miss Burt—lovely, alluring little Dorothy Burt—was not the hardened criminal for whom he was looking!

Then it came back to Schuyler. No! Never Schuyler! But if not he, then who? And what was he doing in that incriminating interval, and why wouldn't he tell?

And then, idly gazing from his window Rob saw again two figures walking in the rose-garden. And they were the same two that he had seen there the evening before.

Schuyler Carleton and Dorothy Burt were strolling,—no, now they were standing, standing close to each other in earnest conversation.

Rob was no eavesdropper, and of course he couldn't hear a word they said, but somehow he found it impossible to take his eyes from those two figures.

Steadily they talked,—so engrossed in their conversation that they scarcely moved; then Schuyler's arm went slowly round the girl's shoulders.

Gently she drew away, and he did not then again offer a caress.

Rob sat looking at them, saying frankly to himself that he was justified in doing so, since his motive effaced all consideration of puerile conventions. If that girl were really the designing young woman he took her to be,—more, if she could be the author, directly or indirectly, of that awful crime,—then Fessenden vowed he would save Schuyler from her fascinations at the risk of breaking their own lifelong friendship.

After further rapt and earnest conversation, Carleton took Miss Burt gently in his arms and kissed her lightly on the forehead. Then, drawing her arm through his own, they turned and walked slowly to the house.

A few moments later Rob heard the girl's light footsteps as she came up to her room, but Carleton stayed down in the library until long after all the rest of the household were sleeping.

XV

FESSENDEN'S DETECTIVE WORK

Next morning Rob went over to the Van Norman house with a clearly developed plan of action. He declared to himself that he would allow no circumstance to shake his faith in his friend, that he would hold Carleton innocent of all wrongdoing in the affair, and that he would put all his ingenuity and cleverness to work to discover the criminal or any clue that might lead to such a discovery.

Although some questions he had wished to ask Cicely Dupuy were yet unanswered, Fessenden had discovered several important facts, and, after being admitted to the house, he looked about him for a quiet spot to sit down and tabulate them in black and white. The florist's men were still in the drawing-room, so he went into the library. Here he found only Mrs. Markham and Miss Morton, who were apparently discussing a question on which they held opposite opinions.

"Come in, Mr. Fessenden," said Mrs. Markham, as he was about to withdraw. "I should be glad of your advice. Ought I to give over the reins of government at once to Miss Morton?"

"Why not?" interrupted Miss Morton, herself. "The house is mine; why should I not be mistress here?"

Fessenden repressed a smile. It seemed to him absurd that these two middle-aged women should discuss an issue of this sort with such precipitancy.

"It seems to me a matter of good taste," he replied. "The house, Miss Morton, is legally yours, but as its mistress, I think you'd show a more gracious manner if you would wait for a time before making any changes in the domestic arrangements."

Apparently undesirous of pursuing the gracious course he recommended, Miss Morton rose abruptly and flounced out of the room.

"Now she's annoyed again," observed Mrs. Markham placidly. "The least little thing sets her off."

"If not intrusive, Mrs. Markham, won't you tell me how it comes about that Miss Morton inherits this beautiful house? Is she a relative of the Van Normans?"

"Not a bit of it. She was Richard Van Norman's sweetheart, years and years and years ago. They had a falling-out, and neither of them ever married. Of course he didn't leave her any of his fortune.

93

But only a short time ago, long after her uncle's death, Madeleine found out about it from some old letters. She determined then to hunt up this Miss Morton, and she did so, and they had quite a correspondence. She came here for the wedding, and Madeleine intended she should make a visit, and intended to give her a present of money when she went away. In the meantime Madeleine had made her will, though I didn't know this until to-day, leaving the place and all her own money to Miss Morton. I'm not surprised at this, for Tom Willard has plenty, and as there was no other heir, I know Madeleine felt that part of her uncle's fortune ought to be used to benefit the woman he had loved in his youth."

"That explains Miss Morton, then," said Fessenden. "But what a peculiar woman she is!"

"Yes, she is," agreed Mrs. Markham, in her serene way. "But I'm used to queer people. Richard Van Norman used to give way to the most violent bursts of temper I ever saw. Maddy and Tom are just like him. They would both fly into furious rages, though I must say they didn't do it often, and never unless for some deep reason."

"And Mr. Carleton—has he a high temper?"

Mrs. Markham's brow clouded. "I don't understand that man," she said slowly. "I don't think he has a quick temper, but there's something deep about him that I can't make out. Oh, Mr. Fessenden, do you think he killed our Madeleine?"

"Do you?" said Fessenden suddenly, looking straight at her.

"I do," she said, taken off her guard. "That is, I couldn't believe it, only, what else can I think? Mr. Carleton is a good man, but I know Maddy never killed herself, and I know the way this house is locked up every night. No burglar or evil-doer could possibly get in."

"But the murderer may have been concealed in the house for hours beforehand."

"Nonsense! That would be impossible, with a house so full of people, and the wedding preparations going on, and everything. Besides, Mr. Hunt would have heard any intruder prowling around; and then again, how could he have gone out? Everything was bolted on the inside, except the front door, and had he gone out that way he must surely have been heard."

"Well reasoned, Mrs. Markham! I think, with you, we may dismiss the possibility of a burglar. The time was too short for anything except a definitely premeditated act. And yet I cannot believe the act was that of Schuyler Carleton. I know that man very well, and a truer, braver soul never existed."

"I know it," declared Mrs. Markham, "but I think I'm justified in telling you this. Mr. Carleton didn't love Madeleine, and he did love another girl. Madeleine worshipped him, and I think he came

94

last night to ask her to release him, and she refused, and then—and then——"

Something about Mrs. Markham's earnest face and sad, distressed voice affected Fessenden deeply, and he wondered if this theory she had so clearly, though hesitatingly, stated, could be the true one. Might he, after all, be mistaken in his estimate of Schuyler Carleton, and might Mrs. Markham's suggestion have even a foundation of probability?

They were both silent for a few minutes, and then Mr. Fessenden said, "But you thought it was suicide at first."

"Indeed I did; I looked at the paper through glasses that were dim with tears, and it looked to me like Madeleine's writing. Of course Miss Morton also thought it was, as she was only slightly familiar with Maddy's hand. But now that we know some one else wrote that message, of course we also know the dear girl did not bring about her own death."

Mrs. Markham was called away on some household errands then, and Fessenden remained alone in the library, trying to think of some clue that would point to some one other than Carleton.

"I'm sure that man is not a murderer," he declared to himself. "Carleton is peculiar, but he has a loyal, honest heart. And yet, if not, who can have done the deed? I can't seem to believe it really was either the Dupuy woman or the Burt girl. And I know it wasn't Schuyler! There must have been some motive of which I know nothing. And perhaps I also know nothing of the murderer. It need not necessarily have been one of these people we have already questioned." His thoughts strayed to the under-servants of the house, to common burglars, or to some powerful unknown villain. But always the thought returned that no one could have entered and left the house unobserved within that fatal hour.

And then, to his intense satisfaction, Kitty French came into the room.

"Good morning, Rose of Dawn," he said, looking at her bright face. "Are you properly glad to see me?"

"Yes, kind sir," she said, dropping a little curtsey, and smiling in a most friendly way.

"Well, then, sit down here, and let me talk to you, for my thoughts are running riot, and I'm sure you alone can help me straighten them out."

"Of course I can. I'm wonderful at that sort of thing. But, first I'll tell you about Miss Dupuy. She's awfully ill—I mean prostrated, you know; and she has a high fever and sometimes she chatters rapidly, and then again she won't open her lips even if any one speaks to her. We've had the doctor, and he says it's just

95

overstrained nerves and a naturally nervous disposition; but, Mr. Fessenden, I think it's more than that; I think it's a guilty conscience."

"And yesterday, when I implied that Miss Dupuy might know more about it all than she admitted, you wouldn't listen to a word of it!"

"Yes, I know it, but I've changed my mind."

"Oh, you have; just for a change, I suppose."

"No," said Kitty, more seriously; "but because I've heard a lot of Cicely's ranting,—for that's what it is,—and while it's been only disconnected sentences and sudden exclamations, yet it all points to a guilty knowledge of some sort, which she's trying to conceal. I don't say I suspect her, Mr. Fessenden, but I do suspect that she knows a lot more important information than she's told."

"Miss Dupuy's behavior has certainly invited criticism," began Rob, but before he could go further, the French girl, Marie, appeared at the door, and seemed about to enter.

"What is it, Marie?" said Kitty kindly. "Are you looking for me?"

"Yes, mademoiselle," said Marie, "and I would speak with monsieur too. I have that to say which is imperative. Too long already have I kept the silence. I must speak at last. Have I permission?"

"Certainly," said Fessenden, who saw that Marie was agitated, but very much in earnest. "Tell us what you have to say. Do not be afraid."

"I am afraid," said Marie, "but I am afraid of one only. It is the Miss Morton, the stranger lady."

"Miss Morton?" said Kitty, in surprise. "She won't hurt you; she has been very good to you."

"Ah, yes, mademoiselle; but too good. Miss Morton has been too kind, too sweet, to Marie! It is that which troubles me."

"Well, out with it, Marie," said Rob. "Close that door, if you like, and then speak out, without any more beating around the bush."

"No, monsieur, I will no longer beat the bush; I will now tell."

Marie carefully closed the door, and then began her story:

"It was the night of the—of the horror. You remember, Miss French, we sat all in this very room, awaiting the coming of the great doctor—the doctor Leonard."

"Yes," said Kitty, looking intently at the girl; "yes, I know most of you stayed here waiting,—but I was not here; Doctor Hills sent Miss Gardner and me to our rooms."

"Yes; it is so. Well, we sat here, and Miss Morton rose with suddenness and left the room. I followed, partly that I thought she might need my services, and partly—I confess it—because I trusted her not at all, and I wished to assure myself that all was well. I followed her,—but secretly,—and I—shall I tell you what she did?"

Kitty hesitated. She was not sure she should listen to what was, after all, servants' gossip about a guest of the house.

But Fessenden looked at it differently. He knew Marie had been the trusted personal maid of Miss Van Norman, and he deemed it right to hear the evidence that she was now anxious to give.

"Go on, Marie," he said gravely. "Be careful to tell it exactly as it happened, whatever it is."

"Yes, m'sieur. Well, then, I softly followed Miss Morton, because she did not go directly to her own room, but went to Miss Van Norman's sitting-room and stood before the desk of Miss Madeleine."

"You are sure, Marie?" said Kitty, who couldn't help feeling it was dishonorable to listen to this.

"Please, Miss French, let her tell the story in her own way," said Rob. "It is perhaps of the utmost importance, and may lead to great results."

Then Marie went uninterruptedly on.

"She stood in front of the desk, m'sieur; she searched eagerly for papers, reading and discarding several. Then she found some, which she saw with satisfaction, and hastily concealed in her pocket. Miss Morton is a lady who yet has pockets in her gowns. With the papers in her pocket, then, Miss Morton looks about carefully, and, thinking herself unobserved, creeps, but stealthily, to her own room. There—m'sieur, I was obliged to peep at the key-hole—there she lighted a fire in her grate, and burned those papers. With my eyes I saw her. Never would I have told, for it was not my affair, but that I fear for Miss Dupuy. It is in the air that she knows secrets concerning Miss Van Norman's death. Ah, if one would know secrets, one should question Miss Morton."

"This is a grave charge you bring against the lady, Marie," said Fessenden.

"Yes, monsieur, but it is true."

"I know it is true," said Kitty; "I have not mentioned it before, but I saw Miss Morton go to Madeleine's room that night, and afterward go to her own room. I knew nothing, of course, of the papers, and so thought little of the whole incident, but if she really took papers from Madeleine's desk and burned them, it's indeed important. What could the papers have been?"

"You know she inherited," began Fessenden.

"Oh, a will!" cried Kitty.

"Marie, you may go now," Rob interrupted; "you did right to tell us this, and rest assured you shall never be blamed for doing so. You

97

will probably be questioned further, but for the present you may go. And thank you."

Marie curtseyed and went away.

"She's a good girl," said Kitty. "I always liked her; and she must have heard, as I did, so much of Cicely's chatter, that she feared some sort of suspicion would fall on Cicely, and she wanted to divert it toward Miss Morton instead."

"As usual, with your quick wits, you've gone right to the heart of her motive," said Rob; "but it may be more serious than you've yet thought of. Miss Morton inherits, you know."

"Yes, now," said Kitty significantly, "since she burnt that other will."

"What other will?"

"Oh, don't you see? The will she burnt was a later one, that didn't give her this house. She burnt it so the earlier one would stand."

"How do you know this?"

"I don't know it, except by common sense! What else would she take from Maddy's desk and burn except a will? And, of course, a will not in her favor, leaving the one that did bequeath the house to her to appear as the latest will."

"Does this line of argument take us any further?" said Rob, so seriously that Kitty began to think.

"You don't mean," she whispered, "that Miss Morton—in order to——"

"To receive her legacy——"

"Could—no, she couldn't! I won't even think of it!"

"But you thought of Miss Dupuy. Miss French, as I told you yesterday, we must think of every possible person, not every probable one. These suggestions are not suspicions—and they harm no one who is innocent."

"I suppose that is so. Well, let us consider Miss Morton then, but of course she didn't really kill Maddy."

"I trust not. But I must say I could sooner believe it of a woman of her type than Miss Dupuy's."

"But Cicely didn't either! Oh, how can you say such dreadful things!"

"We won't say them any more. They are dreadful. But I thought you were going to help me in my detective work, and you balk at every turn."

"No, I won't," said Kitty, looking repentant. "I do want to help you; and if you'll let me help, I'll suspect everybody you want me to."

"I want you to help me, but this story of Marie's is too big for me to handle by myself. I must put that into Mr. Benson's hands. It is really more important than you can understand."

"I suppose so," said Kitty, so humbly that Rob smiled at her, and had great difficulty to refrain from kissing her.

XVI

SEARCHING FOR CLUES

Believing that Marie's information about Miss Morton was of deep interest, Rob started off at once to confer with Coroner Benson about it.

As he walked along he discussed the affair with himself, and was shocked to realize that for the third time he was suspecting a woman of the murder.

"But how can I help it?" he thought impatiently. "The house was full of women, and not a man in it except the servants, and no breath of suspicion has blown their way. And if a woman did do it, that unpleasant Morton woman is by far the most likely suspect. And if she was actuated by a desire to get her inheritance, why, there's the motive, and she surely had opportunity. It's a tangle, but we must find something soon to guide us. A murder like that can't have been done without leaving some trace somewhere of the criminal." And then Fessenden's thoughts drifted away to Kitty French, and he was quite willing to turn the responsibility of his new information over to Mr. Benson. On his way to the coroner's office he passed the Mapleton Inn. An impulse came to him to investigate Tom Willard's statements, and he turned back and entered the small hotel.

He thought it wiser to be frank in the matter than to attempt to obtain underhand information. Asking to speak with the proprietor alone, he said plainly:

"I'm a detective from New York City, and my name is Fessenden. I'm interested in investigating the death of Miss Van Norman. I have no suspicions of any one in particular, but I'm trying to collect a few absolute facts by way of making a beginning. I wish you, therefore, to consider this conversation confidential."

Mr. Taylor, the landlord of the inn, was flattered at being a party to a confidential conversation with a real detective, and willingly promised secrecy in the matter.

"Then," went on Fessenden, "will you tell me all you know of the movements of Mr. Willard last evening?"

Mr. Taylor looked a bit disappointed at this request, for he foresaw that his story would be but brief. However, he elaborated the recital and spun it out as long as he possibly could. But after all his circumlocution, Fessenden found that the facts were given precisely as Willard had stated them himself.

The bellboy who had carried up the suitcase was called in, and his story also agreed.

"Yessir," said the boy; "I took up his bag, and he gimme a quarter, just like any nice gent would. 'N'en I come downstairs, and after while the gent's bell rang, and I went up, and he wanted ice water. He was in his shirt sleeves then, jes' gittin' ready for bed. So I took up the water, and he said, 'Thank you,' real pleasant-like, and gimme a dime. He's a awful nice man, he is. He had his shoes off that time, 'most ready for bed. And that's all I know about it."

All this was nothing more nor less than Fessenden had expected. He had asked the questions merely for the satisfaction of having verbal corroboration of Tom's own story.

With thanks to Mr. Taylor, and a more material token of appreciation to the boy, he went away.

On reaching the coroner's office, he was told that Mr. Benson was not in. Fessenden was sorry, for he wanted to discuss the Morton episode with him. He thought of going to Lawyer Peabody's, who would know all about Miss Van Norman's will, but as he sauntered through one of the few streets the village possessed, he was rather pleased than otherwise to see Kitty French walking toward him.

She greeted him with apparent satisfaction, and said chummily, "Let's walk along together and talk it over."

Immediately coroner and lawyer faded from Rob's mind, he willingly fell into step beside her, and they walked along the street which soon merged itself into a pleasant country road.

Fessenden told Kitty of his conversation at the inn, but she agreed that it was unimportant.

"Of course," she said, "I suppose it was a good thing to have some one else say the same as Tom said, but as Tom wasn't even in the house, I don't see as he is in the mystery at all. But there's no use of looking further for the criminal. It was Schuyler Carleton, just as sure as I stand here."

Kitty very surely stood there. They had paused beneath an old willow tree by the side of the road, and Kitty, leaning against a rail fence, looked like a very sweet and winsome Portia, determined to mete out justice.

Though he was himself convinced that he was an unprejudiced seeker after truth, at that moment Robert Fessenden found himself very much swayed by the opinions of the pretty, impetuous girl who addressed him.

"I believe I'm going to work all wrong," he declared. "I can't help feeling sure that Carleton didn't do it, and so I'm trying to discover who did."

101

"Well, why is that wrong?" demanded Kitty wonderingly.

"Why, I think a better way to do would be to assume, if only for sake of argument, as they say, or rather for sake of a starting-point—to assume that you are right and that Carleton is the evil-doer, though I swear I don't believe it."

Kitty laughed outright. "You're a nice detective!" she said. "Are you assuming that Schuyler is the villain, merely to be polite to me?"

"I am not, indeed! I feel very politely inclined toward you, I'll admit, but in this matter I'm very much in earnest. And I believe, by assuming that Carleton is the man, and then looking for proof of it, we may run across clues that will lead us to the real villain."

Kitty looked at him admiringly, and for Kitty French to look at any young man admiringly was apt to be a bit disturbing to the young man's peace of mind.

It proved so in this case, and though Fessenden whispered to his own heart that he would attend first to the vindication of his friend Carleton, his own heart whispered back that after that, Miss French must be considered.

"And so," said Rob, as they turned back homeward, "I'm going to work upon this line. I'm going to look for clues; real, material, tangible clues, such as criminals invariably leave behind them."

"Do!" cried Kitty. "And I'll help you. I know we can find something."

"You see," went on Fessenden, his enthusiasm kindling from hers, "the actual stage of the tragedy is so restricted. Whatever we find must be in the Van Norman house."

"Yes, and probably in the library."

"Or the hall," he supplemented.

"What kind of a thing do you expect to find?"

"I don't know, I'm sure. In the Sherlock Holmes stories it's usually cigar ashes or something like that. Oh, pshaw! I don't suppose we'll find anything."

"I think in detective stories everything is found out by footprints. I never saw anything like the obliging way in which people make footprints for detectives."

"And how absurd it is!" commented Rob. "I don't believe footprints are ever made clearly enough to deduce the rest of the man from."

"Well, you see, in detective stories, there's always that 'light snow which had fallen late the night before.'"

"Yes," said Fessenden, laughing at her cleverness, "and there's always some minor character who chances to time that snow exactly, and who knows when it began and when it stopped."

"Yes, and then the principal characters carefully plant their footprints, going and returning—over-lapping, you know—and so Mr. Smarty-Cat Detective deduces the whole story."

"But we've no footprints to help us."

"No, we couldn't have, in the house."

"But if it was Schuyler——"

"Well, even if,—he couldn't make footprints without that convenient 'light snow' and there isn't any."

"And besides, Schuyler didn't do it."

"No, I know he didn't. But you're going to assume that, you know, in order to detect the real criminal."

"Yes, I know I said so; but I don't believe that game will work, after all."

"I don't believe you're much of a detective, any way," said Kitty, so frankly that Fessenden agreed.

"I don't believe I am," he said honestly. "With the time, place, and number of people so limited, it ought to be easy to solve this mystery at once."

"I think it's just those very conditions that make it so hard," said Kitty, sighing.

And so completely under her spell was Fessenden by this time that he emphatically agreed with her.

When they reached the Van Norman house they found it had assumed the hollow, breathless air that invades a house where death is present.

All traces of decoration had been removed from the drawing-room, and it, like the library, had been restored to its usual immaculate order. The scent of flowers, however, was all through the atmosphere, and a feeling of oppression hovered about like a heavy cloud.

Involuntarily Kitty slipped her hand in Rob's as they entered.

Fessenden, too, felt the gloom of the place, but he had made up his mind to do some practical work, and detaining Harris, who had opened the door for them, he said at once, "I want you to open the blinds for a time in all the rooms downstairs. Miss French and I are about to make a search, and, unless necessary, let no one interrupt us."

"Very good, sir," said the impassive Harris, who was becoming accustomed to sudden and unexpected orders.

They had chosen their time well for the search, and were not interrupted. Most of the members of the household were in their own rooms; and there happened to be no callers who entered the house.

Molly Gardner had gone away early that morning. She had

103

declared that if she stayed longer she should be downright ill, and, after vainly trying to persuade Kitty to go with her, had returned alone to New York.

Tom Willard and Lawyer Peabody were in Madeleine's sitting-room, going over the papers in her desk, in a general attempt to learn anything of her affairs that might be important to know. They had desired Miss Dupuy's presence and assistance, but that young woman refused to go to them, saying she was still too indisposed, and remained, under care of Marie, in her own room.

Fessenden suggested that Kitty should make search in the library while he did the same in the drawing-room; and that afterward they should change places.

Kitty shivered a little as she went into the room that had been the scene of the tragedy, but she was really anxious to assist Fessenden, and also she wanted to do anything, however insignificant, that would help in the least toward avenging poor Maddy's death.

And yet it was seemingly a hopeless task. Though she carefully and systematically scrutinized walls, rugs and furniture, not a clue could she find.

She was on her hands and knees under a table when Tom Willard came into the room.

"What are you doing?" he said, unable to repress a smile as Kitty, with her curly hair a bit dishevelled, came scrambling out.

"Hunting for clues," she said briefly.

"There are no clues," said Tom gravely. "It's the most inexplicable affair all 'round."

"Then you have no suspicion of any one?"

"My dear Miss French," said Tom, looking at her kindly, as one might at a child, but speaking decidedly; "don't let the amusement of amateur detective work lead you into making unnecessary trouble for people. If detective work is to be done, leave it to experienced and professional hands. A girl hunting for broken sleeve-links or shreds of clothing is foolishly theatrical."

Willard's grave but gentle voice made Kitty think that she and Fessenden were acting childishly, but after Tom, who had come on an errand, had left the room, Kitty confided to herself that she would rather act foolishly at Rob Fessenden's bidding than to follow the wise advice of any other man.

This was saying a good deal, but as she said it only to herself, she felt sure her confidence would not be betrayed.

Not half an hour had elapsed when Kitty appeared at the drawing-room door with a discontented face, and said, "There's positively nothing in the library that doesn't belong there. It has been thoroughly swept, and though there may have been many clues, they've all been swept and dusted away."

"Same here," said Fessenden dejectedly. "However, let's change rooms, so we can both feel sure." Then Kitty searched the drawing-room, and Rob the library, and they both scrutinized every inch of the hall.

"I didn't find so much as a thread," said Kitty, as they sat down on a great carved seat in the hall to compare notes.

"I didn't either," said Rob, "with one insignificant exception; in the drawing-room I found this, but it doesn't mean anything."

As he spoke he drew from his pocket a tiny globule of a silver color.

"What is it?" asked Kitty, taking it with her finger-tips from the palm of his hand.

"It's a cachou."

"And what in the world is a cachou? What is it for?"

"Why, it's a little confection filled with a sort of spice. Some men use them after smoking, to eradicate the odor of tobacco."

"Eat them, do you mean? Are they good to eat?" and impulsive Kitty was about to pop the tiny thing into her mouth, when Rob caught her hand.

"Don't!" he cried. "That's my only clue, after all this search, and it may be of importance."

He rescued the cachou from Kitty's fingers, and then, slipping it into his pocket, he continued to hold the hand from which he had taken it.

And then, somehow, detective work seemed for a moment to lose its intense interest, and Rob and Kitty talked of other things.

Suddenly Kitty said: "Tom Willard thinks we're foolish to hunt for clues."

"I think he's right," said Fessenden, smiling, "since we didn't find anything."

"Oh, he didn't exactly say you were foolish, but he said I was. He said it was silly for a girl to hunt around under tables and chairs."

"He had no right to say so. It isn't silly for you to do anything you want to do. But I know what Willard meant. He thinks, as lots of people do, that there's no sense in expecting to find material evidences of crime—or, rather, of the criminal. And I suppose he's right. Whoever murdered Miss Van Norman certainly left no tangible traces. But I'm glad we hunted for them, for now I feel certain there were none left; otherwise, I should always have thought there might have been."

"How much more sensible you are than Mr. Willard," said

Kitty, with an admiring glance that went straight to the young man's heart, and stayed there. "And, too, you always make use of 'clues' if you do find them. Look how cleverly you deduced about the soft and hard lead pencils."

"Oh, that was nothing," said Fessenden modestly, though her praise was ecstasy to his soul.

"Indeed it was something! It was great work. And I truly believe you'll make as great a deduction from that little thing you found this morning. What do you call it?"

"A cachou."

"Yes, a cachou. The whole discovery of the murderer may hinge on that tiny clue we found."

"It may, but I can hardly hope so."

"I hope so,—for I do want to prove to Tom Willard that our search for clues wasn't silly, after all."

And Fessenden's foolish heart was so joyed at Kitty's use of "we" and "our" that he cared not a rap for Willard's opinion of his detective methods.

106

XVII

MISS MORTON'S STATEMENTS

That afternoon another session of the inquest was held.

Fessenden had told Coroner Benson of Marie's disclosures concerning Miss Morton, and in consequence that lady was the first witness called.

The summons was a complete surprise to her. Turning deathly white, she endeavored to answer to her name, but only gave voice to an unintelligible stammer.

The coroner spoke gently, realizing that his feminine cloud of witnesses really gave him a great deal of trouble.

"Please tell us, Miss Morton," he said, "what was your errand when you left the library and went upstairs, remaining there nearly half an hour, on the night of Miss Van Norman's death?"

"I didn't do any such thing!" snapped Miss Morton, and though her tone was defiant now, her expression still showed fear and dismay.

"You must have forgotten. Think a moment. You were seen to leave the library, and you were also seen after you reached the upper floors. So try to recollect clearly, and state your errand upstairs at that time."

"I—I was overcome at the tragedy of the occasion, and I went to my own room to be alone for a time."

"Did you go directly from the library to your own room?"

"Yes."

"Without stopping in any other room on the way?"

"Yes."

"Think again, please. Perhaps I had better tell you, a witness has already told of your stopping on the way to your own room."

"She told falsely, then. I went straight to my bedroom."

"In the third story?"

"Yes."

Coroner Benson was a patient man. He had no wish to confound Miss Morton with Marie's evidence, and too, there was a chance that Marie had not told the truth. So he spoke again persuasively:

"You went there afterward, but first you stopped for a moment or two in Miss Van Norman's sitting-room."

"Who says I did?"

"An eye-witness, who chanced to see you."

"Chanced to see me, indeed! Nothing of the sort! It was that little French minx, Marie, who is everlastingly spying about! Well, she is not to be believed."

"I am sorry to doubt your own statement, Miss Morton, but another member of the household also saw you. Denial is useless; it would be better for you to tell us simply why you went to Miss Van Norman's room at that time."

"It's nobody's business," snapped Miss Morton. "My errand there had nothing to do in any way with Madeleine Van Norman, dead or alive."

"Then, there is no reason you should not tell frankly what that errand was."

"I have my own reasons, and I refuse to tell."

Mr. Benson changed his tactics.

"Miss Morton," he said, "when did you first know that you were to inherit this house and also a considerable sum of money at the death of Miss Van Norman?"

The effect of this sudden question was startling. Miss Morton seemed to be taken off her guard. She turned red, then paled to a sickly white. Once or twice she essayed to speak, but hesitated and did not do so.

"Come, come," said the coroner, "that cannot be a difficult question to answer. When was your first intimation that you were a beneficiary by the terms of Miss Van Norman's will?"

And now Miss Morton had recovered her bravado.

"When the will was read," she said in cold, firm accents.

"No; you knew it before that. You learned it when you went to Miss Van Norman's room and read some papers which were in her desk. You read from a small private memorandum book that she had bequeathed this place to you at her death."

"Nothing of the sort," returned the quick, snappy voice. "I knew it before that."

"And you just said you learned of it first when the will was read!"

"Well, I forgot. Madeleine told me the day I came here last year that she had made a will leaving the house to me, because she thought it should have been mine any way."

"The day you were here last year, she told you this?"

"Yes, we had a little conversation on the subject, and she told me."

"Why did you not say this when I first asked you concerning the matter?"

"I forgot it." Miss Morton spoke nonchalantly, as if contradicting oneself was a matter of no moment.

"Then you knew of your legacy before Miss Van Norman died?"

"Yes, now that I think of it, I believe I did."

She was certainly a difficult witness. She seemed unable to look upon the questions as important, and her answers were given either in a flippant or savage manner.

"Then why did you go to Miss Van Norman's room to look for her will that night?"

"Her will? I didn't!"

"No, not the will that bequeathed you the house, but a later will that made a different disposal of it."

"There wasn't such a one," said Miss Morton, in a low, scared voice.

"What, then, was the paper which you took from Miss Van Norman's desk, carried to your own room, and burned?"

The coroner's voice was not persuasive now; it was accusing, and his face was stern as he awaited her reply.

Again Miss Morton's face blanched to white. Her thin lips formed a straight line, and her eyes fell, but her voice was strong and sibilant, as she fairly hissed:

"How dare you! Of what do you accuse me?"

"Of burning a paper which you took secretly from Miss Van Norman's private desk."

A moment's hesitation, and then, "I did not do it," she said clearly.

"But you were seen to do it."

"By whom?"

"By a disinterested and credible witness."

"By a sly, spying French servant!"

"It matters not by whom; you are asked to explain the act of burning that paper."

"I have nothing to explain. I deny it."

And try as he would Mr. Benson could not prevail upon Miss Morton to admit that she had burned a paper.

He confronted her with the witness, Marie, but Miss Morton coldly refused to listen to her, or to pay any attention to what she said. She insisted that Marie was not speaking the truth, and as the matter rested between the two, there was nothing more to be done.

Kitty French said that she saw Miss Morton go into Madeleine's room, and afterward go upstairs to her own room, but she knew nothing about the papers in question.

Still adhering to her denial of Marie's story, Miss Morton was excused from the witness stand.

Another witness called was Dorothy Burt. Fessenden was sorry

109

that this had to be, for he dreaded to have the fact of Carleton's infatuation for this girl brought into public notice.

Miss Burt was a model witness, as to her manner and demeanor. She answered promptly and clearly all the coroner's questions, and at first Rob thought that perhaps she was, after all, the innocent child that Carleton thought her.

But he couldn't help realizing, as the cross-questioning went on, that Miss Burt really gave very little information of any value. Perhaps because she had none to give, perhaps because she chose to withhold it.

"Your name?" Mr. Benson had first asked.

"Dorothy Burt," was the answer, and the modest voice, with a touch of sadness, as befitting the occasion, seemed to have just the right ring to it.

"Your occupation?"

"I am companion and social secretary to Mrs. Carleton."

"Do you know of anything that can throw any light on any part of the mystery surrounding the death of Miss Van Norman?"

Miss Burt drew her pretty eyebrows slightly together, and thought a moment.

"No," she said quietly; "I am sure I do not."

So gentle and sweet was she, that many a questioner would have dismissed her then and there; but Mr. Benson, hoping to get at least a shred of evidence bearing on Schuyler Carleton's strange behavior, continued to question her.

"Tell us, please, Miss Burt, what you know of Mr. Carleton's actions on the night of Miss Van Norman's death."

"Mr. Carleton's actions?" The delicate eyebrows lifted as if in perplexity at the question.

"Yes; detail his actions, so far as you know them, from the time he came home to dinner that evening."

"Why, let me see;" pretty Dorothy looked thoughtful again. "He came to dinner, as usual. Mr. Fessenden was there, but no other guest. After dinner we all sat in the music room. I played a little,— just some snatches of certain music that Mrs. Carleton is fond of. Mr. Carleton and Mr. Fessenden chatted together."

Rob raised his own eyebrows a trifle at this. Carleton had not been at all chatty; indeed, Fessenden and Mrs. Carleton had sustained the burden of the conversation; and while Miss Burt had played, it had been bits of romantic music that Rob felt sure had been for Schuyler's delectation more than his mother's.

"Is that all?" said Mr. Benson.

"Yes, I think so," said Miss Burt; "we all went to our rooms

110

early, as the next day was the day appointed for Mr. Carleton's wedding, and we assumed he wanted to be alone."

Rob looked up astounded. Was she going to make no mention of the stroll in the rose-garden? He almost hoped she wouldn't, and yet that was certainly the evidence Mr. Benson was after.

"You said good-night to Mr. Carleton at what time, then?" was the next rather peculiar question.

It might have been imagination, but Fessenden thought the girl was going to name an earlier hour, then, catching sight of Rob's steady eyes upon her, she hesitated an instant, and then said: "About ten o'clock, I think."

"Mrs. Carleton and Mr. Fessenden went to their rooms at the same time?"

Dorothy Burt turned very pale. She shot a quick glance at Schuyler Carleton and another at Fessenden, and then said in a low tone: "They had gone upstairs a short time before."

"And you remained downstairs for a time with Mr. Carleton?"

"Yes." The answer, merely a whisper, seemed forced upon her lips.

"Where were you?"

Again the hesitation. Again the swift glances at Carleton and Rob, and then the low answer:

"In the rose-garden."

Fessenden understood. The girl had no desire to tell these things, but she knew that he knew the truth, and so she was too clever to lie uselessly.

"How long were you two in the rose-garden, Miss Burt?"

Another pause. Somehow, Fessenden seemed to see the workings of the girl's mind. If she designated a long time it would seem important. If too short a time, Rob would know of her inaccuracy. And if she said she didn't know, it would lend a meaning to the rose-garden interview which it were better to avoid.

"Perhaps a half-hour," she said, at last, and, though outwardly calm, her quickly-drawn breath and shining eyes betokened a suppressed excitement of some sort.

"And you left Mr. Carleton at ten o'clock?"

"Yes."

"Do you know what he did after that?"

"I do not!" the answer rang out clearly, as if Miss Burt were glad to be well past the danger point of the dialogue. But it came back at her with the next question.

"What was the tenor of your conversation with Mr. Carleton in the rose garden?"

At this Dorothy Burt's calm gave way. She trembled, her red

111

lower lip quivered, and her eye-lids fluttered, almost as if she were about to faint.

But, by a quick gesture, she straightened herself up, and, looking her interlocutor in the eyes said:

"I trust I am not obliged to answer that very personal question."

Like a flash it came to Fessenden that her perturbation had been merely a clever piece of acting. She had trembled and seemed greatly distressed in order that Mr. Benson's sympathy might be so aroused that he would not press the question.

And indeed it required a hardened heart to insist on an answer from the lovely, agitated girl.

But Mr. Benson was not so susceptible as some younger men, and, moreover, he was experienced in the ways of witnesses.

"I am sorry to be so personal, Miss Burt," he said firmly; "but I fear it is necessary for us to learn the purport of your talk with Mr. Carleton at that time."

Dorothy Burt looked straight at Schuyler Carleton.

Neither gave what might be called a gesture, and yet a message and a response flashed between the two.

Rob Fessenden, watching intently, translated it to mean a simple negative on Schuyler's part, but the question in the girl's eyes he could not read.

Carleton's "No," however, was as plain as if spoken, and, apparently comprehending, Miss Burt went evenly on.

"We talked," she said, "on such subjects as might be expected on the eve of a man's wedding-day. We discussed the probability of pleasant weather, mention was made of Miss Van Norman and her magnificent personality. The loneliness of Mrs. Carleton after her son's departure was touched upon, and, while I cannot remember definitely, I think our whole talk was on those or kindred topics."

"Why did you so hesitate a moment ago, when I asked you to tell this?"

Dorothy opened her lovely eyes in surprise.

"Hesitate! Why, I didn't. Why should I?"

Mr. Benson was at last put to rout. She had hesitated—more than hesitated; she had been distinctly averse to relating what she now detailed as a most indifferent conversation, but, in the face of that expression of injured innocence, Mr. Benson could say no more on that subject.

"When you left Mr. Carleton," he went on, "did you know he was about to come over here to Miss Van Norman's?"

Again the telegraphic signals between Miss Burt and Carleton.

Quick as a flash—invisible to most of the onlookers, but distinctly seen by Fessenden—a question was asked and answered.

112

"No," she said quickly; "I did not."

"You left him at ten o'clock, then, and did not see him again that night?"

"That is correct."

"And you have no idea how he was occupied from ten o'clock, on?"

"I have not."

"That's all at present, Miss Burt."

The girl left the witness-stand looking greatly troubled.

But the suspicious Mr. Fessenden firmly believed she looked troubled because it made her more prettily pathetic.

He wasn't entirely right in this, but neither was Dorothy Burt quite as ingenuous as she appeared.

XVIII

CARLETON IS FRANK

Nearly a week had passed.

The funeral of Madeleine Van Norman had been such as befitted the last of the name, and she had been reverently laid away to rest in the old family vault.

But the mystery of her death was not yet cleared up. The coroner's inquest had been finished, but most of the evidence, though vaguely indicative, had been far from conclusive.

No further witnesses had been found, and no further important fact had been discovered.

Schuyler Carleton maintained the same inscrutable air, and, though often nervous to the verge of collapse, had reiterated his original story over and over again without deviation. He still refused to state his errand to the Van Norman house on the night of Madeleine's death. He still declined to say what he was doing between the time he entered the house and the time when he cried out for help. He himself asserted there was little, if any, time therein unaccounted for.

Tom Willard, of course, repeated his story, and it was publicly corroborated by witnesses from the hotel. Tom had changed some during these few days. The sudden accession of a large fortune seemed to burden him rather than to bring him joy. But no one wondered at this when they remembered the sad circumstances which gave him his wealth, and remembered, too, what was no secret to anybody, that he had deeply loved his cousin Madeleine. Of the other witnesses, Cicely Dupuy was the only one whose later evidence was not entirely in accordance with her earlier statements. She often contradicted herself, and when in the witness chair was subject to sudden fainting attacks, whether real or assumed no one was quite sure.

And so, after the most exhaustive inquiry and the most diligent sifting of evidence, the jury could return only the time-worn verdict, "Death at the hands of some person or persons unknown."

But in addition to this it was recommended by the jury that Schuyler Carleton be kept under surveillance. There had not been enough evidence to warrant his arrest, but the district attorney was so convinced of the man's guilt that he felt sure proofs of it would sooner or later be brought to light.

Carleton himself seemed apathetic in the matter. He quite

realized that his guilt was strongly suspected by most of the community, but, instead of breaking down under this, he seemed rather to accept it sadly and without dispute.

But though the inquest itself was over, vigorous investigation was going on. A detective of some reputation had the case in hand officially, and, unlike many celebrated detectives, he was quite willing to confer with or to be advised by young Fessenden.

Spurred by the courtesy and confidence of his superior, Rob devoted himself with energy to the work of unravelling the mystery, but it was baffling work. As he confessed to Kitty French, who was in all things his confidante, every avenue of argument led up against a blank wall.

"Either Carleton did do or he did not," he said reflectively. "If he did, there's absolutely no way we can prove it; and if he didn't, who did?"

Kitty agreed that this was a baffling situation.

"What about that cachou, or whatever you call it?" she said.

"It didn't amount to anything as a clue," returned Rob moodily. "I showed it to some of the servants, and they said they had never seen such a thing before. Harris was quite sure that none of the men who came here ever use them. I asked Carleton, just casually, for one the other day, and he said he didn't have any and never had had any. I asked Willard for one at another time, and he said the same thing. It must have been dropped by some of the decorator's men; they seemed a Frenchy crowd, and I've been told the French are addicted to these things." Rob took the tiny silver sphere from his pocket and looked at it as he talked. "Besides, it wouldn't mean a thing if it had belonged to anybody. I just picked it up because it was the only thing I could find in the drawing-room that wasn't too heavy to lift."

Rob put his useless clue back into his pocket with a sigh. "I'm going to give it up," he said, "and go back to New York. I've stayed here in Mapleton over a week now, hoping I could be of some help to poor old Carleton; but I can't—and yet I know he's innocent! Fairbanks, the detective on the case, is pleasant to work with, and I like him; but if he can't find out anything, of course I needn't hope to. I'd stay on, though, if I thought Carleton cared to have me. But I'm not sure he does, so I'm going back home. When are you going to New York, Kitty?"

But the girl did not answer his question. "Rob," she said, for the intimacy between these two young people had reached the stage of first names, "I have an inspiration."

"I wish I had some faith in it, my dear girl; but your inspirations have such an inevitable way of leading up a tree."

"I know it, and this may also. But listen: doesn't Schuyler believe that you suspect him?"

"I don't suspect him," declared Rob, almost fiercely.

"I know you don't; but doesn't Schuyler think you do?"

"Why, I don't know; I never thought about it. I think very likely he does."

"And he's so proud, of course he won't discuss it with you, or justify himself in any way. Now, look here, Rob: you go to Schuyler, and in your nicest, friendliest way tell him you don't believe he did it. Then—don't you see?—if he is innocent, he will expand and confide in you, and you may get a whole lot of useful information. And on the other hand, if he is guilty, you'll probably learn the fact from his manner."

Rob thought it over. "Kitty," he said at last, "you're a trump. I believe you have hit upon the only thing there is to try, and I'll try it before I decide to go to New York. I'll stay in Mapleton a day or two longer, for the more I think about it, the more I think I haven't been fair or just to the old boy in not even asking for his confidence."

"It isn't that so much, but you must assure him of your belief in him. Tell him you know he is innocent."

"I do know it."

"Yes, I know that has been your firm conviction all along, though it isn't mine. But don't tell him it isn't mine; just tell him of your own confidence and sympathy and faith in him, and see what happens."

"A woman's intuitions are always ahead of a man's," declared Rob heartily. "I'll do just as you say, Kitty, and I'll do it wholeheartedly, and to the best of my ability."

Kitty was still staying in the Van Norman house, which had not yet been, and probably would not soon be, known by any other name.

Mrs. Markham had gone away temporarily, though it was believed that when she returned it would be merely to arrange for her permanent departure. The good lady had received a generous bequest in Madeleine's will, and, except for the severing of old associations, she had no desire to remain in a house no longer the home of the Van Normans.

Miss Morton was therefore mistress of the establishment, and thoroughly did she enjoy her position. She invited Miss French to remain for a time as her visitor, and Kitty had stayed on, in hope of learning the truth about the tragedy.

At Miss Morton's invitation Tom Willard had left the hotel and returned to his old room, which he had given up to Miss Morton herself at Madeleine's request.

Willard without doubt sorrowed deeply for his beautiful cousin, but he was a man who rarely gave voice to his grief, and his feelings were evident more from his manner than his words. He seemed preoccupied and absent-minded, and, quite unlike Miss Morton, he was in no haste to take even preliminary steps toward the actual acquisition of his fortune.

Fessenden was curious to know whether Willard suspected that his cousin's death was the work of Schuyler Carleton. But when he tried to sound Tom on the subject he was met by a rebuff. It was politely worded, but it was nevertheless a plain-spoken rebuff, and conclusively forbade further discussion of the subject.

And so as an outcome of Kitty's suggestion, Fessenden determined to have a plain talk with Schuyler Carleton.

"Old man," he said, the first time opportunity found him alone with Schuyler in the Carleton library, "I want to offer you my help. I know that sounds presumptuous, but we're old friends, Carleton, and I think I may be allowed a little presumption on that score. And first, though it seems to me absurdly unnecessary, I want to assure you of my belief in your own innocence. Pshaw, belief is a weak word! I know, I am positive, that you no more killed that girl than I did!"

The light that broke over Carleton's countenance was a fine vindication of Kitty's theory. The weary, drawn look disappeared from his face, and, impulsively grasping Rob's hand, he exclaimed, "Do you mean that?"

"Of course I mean it. I never for an instant thought it possible. You're not that sort of a man."

"Not that sort of a man;" Carleton spoke musingly. "That isn't the point, Fessenden. I've thought this thing out pretty thoroughly, and I must say I don't wonder that they suspect me of the deed. You see, it's a case of exclusive opportunity."

"That phrase always makes me tired," declared Rob. "If there's one thing more misleading than 'circumstantial evidence,' it is 'exclusive opportunity.' Now, look here, Carleton, if you'll let me, I'm going to take up this matter. Should you be arrested and tried— and I may as well tell you frankly I'm pretty sure that you will be—I want to act as your lawyer. But in the meantime I want to endeavor to track down the real murderer and so leave no occasion for your trial."

Schuyler Carleton looked like a condemned man who has just been granted a reprieve.

"Do you know, Fessenden," he said, "you're the only one who does believe me innocent?"

"Nonsense, man! Nobody believes you guilty."

117

"They're so strongly suspicious that it's little short of belief," said Carleton sadly. "And truly, Rob, I can't blame them. Everything is against me."

"I admit there are some things that must be explained away; and, Schuyler, if I'm to be your lawyer, or, rather, since I am your lawyer, I must ask you to be perfectly frank with me."

Carleton looked troubled. He was not of a frank nature, and it was always difficult for him to confide his personal affairs to anybody. Fessenden saw this, and resolved upon strong measures.

"You must tell me everything," he said somewhat sternly. "You must do this at the sacrifice of your own wishes. You must ignore yourself, and lay your whole heart bare to me, for the sake of your mother, and—for the sake of the woman you love."

Schuyler Carleton started as if he had been physically struck.

"What do you mean?" he cried.

"You know what I mean," said Fessenden gently. "You did not love the woman you were about to marry. You do love another. Can you deny it?"

"No," said Carleton, settling back into his apathy. "And since you know that, I may as well tell you all. I admired and respected Madeleine Van Norman, and when I asked her to marry me I thought I loved her. After that I met some one else. You know this?"

"Yes; Miss Burt."

"Yes. She came into this house as my mother's companion, and almost from the first time I saw her I knew that she and not Madeleine was the one woman in the world for me. But, Fessenden, never by word or look did I betray this to Miss Burt while Madeleine lived. If she guessed it, it was only because of her woman's intuition. I was always loyal to Madeleine in word and deed, if I could not be in thought."

"Was it not your duty to tell Madeleine this?"

"I tried several times to do so, but, though I hate to sound egotistical, she loved me very deeply, and I felt that honor bound me to her."

"I'm not here to preach to you, and that part of it is, of course, not my affair. I know your nature, and I know that you were as loyal to Miss Van Norman as you would have been had you never seen Miss Burt, and I honor and respect you for it. But you were jealous of Willard?"

"My nature is insanely jealous, yes. And though he was her cousin, I knew Willard was desperately in love with her, and somehow it always made me frantic to see him showing affection toward the woman I meant to make my wife."

"She was not in love with Willard?"

118

"Not in the least. Madeleine's heart beat only for me, ungrateful wretch that I am. Her little feints at flirting with Willard were only to pique me. I knew this, and yet to see them together always roused that demon of jealousy which I cannot control. Fessenden, aside from all else, how can people think I killed the woman who loved me as she did?"

"Of course that argument appeals to you, and of course it does to me. But you must see how others, not appreciating all this, and even suspecting or surmising that your heart was not entirely with your intended bride—you must see that some appearances, at least, are against you."

"I do see; and I see it so plainly that even to me those appearances seem conclusive of my guilt."

"Never mind what they seem to you, old man; they don't seem so to me, and now I'm going to get to work. First, as I told you, you are going to be frank with me. What were you doing in the Van Norman house before you went into the library?"

Schuyler Carleton blushed. It was not the shame of a guilty man, but the embarrassment of one detected in some betrayal of sentiment.

"Of course I will tell you," he said after a moment. "I went there on an errand which I wished to keep entirely secret. There is a foolish superstition in our family that has been observed for many generations. An old reliquary which was blessed by some ancient Pope has been handed down from father to son for many generations. The superstition is that unless this ancient trinket hangs over the head of a bridegroom on his wedding day, ill fortune will follow him through life. It is part of the superstition that the reliquary must be put in place secretly, and especially without the knowledge of the bride, else its charm is broken. The whole notion is foolishness, but as my wedding was an ill-starred one, any way, I hoped to gain happiness, if possible, by this means. Of course, I don't think I really had any faith in the thing, but it is such an old tradition in the family that it never occurred to me not to follow it. My mother gave me the reliquary, after my father's death, telling me the history of it. I had it with me when I was at the house in the afternoon, and I hoped to find an opportunity to fasten it up in that floral bower, unobserved. But the workmen were busy there when I came away, and I knew there would be many people about the next morning; so I decided to return late at night to do my errand. I had no thought of seeing Madeleine. There were no bright lights in the house, and the drawing-room itself was dark save for what light came in from the hall. I did go into the house, I suppose, at about quarter after eleven. I didn't note the time, but I dare say Mr. Hunt

119

was correct. Without glancing toward the library then, I went at once to the drawing-room and hid the reliquary among the garlands that formed the top of that bower. As I stood there, I thought over what I was about to do the next day. It seemed to me that I was doing right, and I vowed to myself to be a true and loving husband to my chosen wife. I stood there some time, thinking, and then turned to go away. As I left the room I noticed a low light in the library, and it occurred to me that if any one should be in there it would be wiser to make my presence known. So I crossed the hall and went into the library. The rest you know. The sudden shock of seeing Madeleine as she was, just as I had come from what was to have been our bridal bower, nearly unhinged my mind. I picked up the dagger, I turned on lights and rang bells, not knowing what I did. Now I have told you the truth, and if my demeanor has seemed strange, can you wonder at it in a man who experienced what I did, and then is suspected of being the criminal?"

"Indeed, no," said Fessenden, grasping his friend's hand in sincere sympathy. "It was a terrible experience, and the injustice of the suspicion resting on you makes it a hundredfold more horrible."

"When I went back to the house next morning I watched for an opportunity, and managed, unobserved, to remove the reliquary from its floral hiding-place. I shall never use it now. There are some men fated not to know happiness, and I am of those."

"Let us hope not," said Fessenden gently. "But whatever the future may hold, let us now keep to the business at hand, and use every possible means to discover the evil-doer."

120

XIX

THE TRUTH ABOUT MISS BURT

Confidential relations thus being established between the two men, Fessenden wished very much to learn a little more concerning Dorothy Burt, but found it a difficult subject to introduce.

It was, therefore, greatly to his satisfaction when Carleton himself led up to it.

"I've been frank with you, Rob," he said, "but perhaps there's one more thing I ought to confess."

"Nonsense, man, I'm not your father confessor. If you've any facts, hand them over, but don't feel that you must justify yourself to me."

"But I do want to tell you this, for it will help you to understand my sensitiveness in the whole matter. As you know, Rob, I do love Dorothy Burt, and it is only since Madeleine's death that I have allowed myself to realize how much I love her. I shall never ask her to marry me, for the stigma of this dreadful affair will always remain attached to my name, and suspicion would more than ever turn to me, if I showed my regard for Dorothy. As I told you, I never spoke a word of love to her while Madeleine was alive. But she knew,—she couldn't help knowing. Brave little girl that she is, she never evinced that knowledge, and it was only when I surprised a sudden look in her eyes that I suspected she too cared for me. And yet, though we never admitted it to each other, Madeleine suspected the truth, and even taxed me with it. Of course I denied it; of course I vowed to Madeleine that she, and she only, was the woman I loved; because I thought it the right and honorable thing to do. If she hadn't cared so much for me herself, I might have asked her to release me; but I never did, and never even thought of doing so—until—that last evening. Then—well, you know how she had favored Willard in preference to me in the afternoon, and, though I well knew it was only to tease me, yet it did tease me, and I came home really angry at her. It was an ill-advised occasion for her to favor her cousin."

"I agree with you; but from the little I know of Miss Van Norman's nature, I judge she was easily piqued and quick to retaliate."

"Yes, she was; we were both too quick to take offense, but, of course, the real reason for that was the lack of true faith between us. Well, then I came home, angered, as I said, and Dorothy was so—so different from Madeleine, so altogether sweet and dear, so free from

121

petty bickering or sarcasm, that for the first time I felt as if I ought not to marry the woman I did not love. I brooded over this thought all through the dinner hour and the early evening. Then you and mother left us, and I asked Dorothy to go for a little stroll in the garden. She refused at first—I think the child was a little fearful of what I might say—but I said nothing of the tumult in my heart. I realized, though, that she knew I loved her, and that—she cared for me. I had thought she did, but never before had I felt so sure of it,—and the knowledge completely unmanned me. I bade her good night abruptly, and rather coldly, and then I went into the library and fought it out with myself. And I concluded that my duty was to Madeleine. I confess to a frantic desire to go to her and ask her, even at that last minute, to free me from my troth, and then I thought what a scandal it would create, and I knew that even if Dorothy and I both suffered, it was Madeleine's right to leave matters as they were. Having decided, I proceeded to carry out my earlier intention of going over to the Van Norman house with the reliquary. It was so late then that I had no thought of seeing Madeleine, but—and this, Rob, is my confession—on the way there, I still had a lingering thought that if I should see Madeleine I would tell her the truth, and leave it to her generosity to set me free. And it was this guilty knowledge—this shameful weakness on my part—that added to my dismay and horror at finding her—as she was, in the library. I read that awful paper,—I thought of course, then, she had taken her own life, and I feared it was because she knew of my falseness and treachery. This made me feel as if I were really her murderer, quite as much as if I had struck the actual blow."

"Don't take it like that, Schuyler; that's morbid imagination. You acted loyally to Miss Van Norman to the last, and though the whole situation was most unfortunate, you were not really to blame. No man can rule his own heart, and, any way, it is not for me to comment on that side of the matter. But since you have spoken thus frankly of Miss Burt, I must ask you how, with your slight acquaintance, you are so sure she is worthy of your regard."

"Our acquaintance isn't so slight, Rob. She has been some time with mother,—more than six months,—and we have been good friends from the first. And I know her, perhaps by Love's intuition,—but I know her very soul,—and she is the truest, sweetest nature God ever made."

"But—forgive me—she has impressed me as being not quite so frank and ingenuous as she appears."

"That's only because you don't know her, and you judge by your own uncertain and mistaken impressions."

"But—when she gave her evidence at the inquest—she seemed

to hesitate, and to waver as to what she should say. It did not have the ring of truth, though her manner was charming and even naïve."

"You misjudge her, Rob. I say this because I know it. And I can't blame you, for, knowing of my engagement to Madeleine, you are quite right to disapprove of my interest in another woman."

"It isn't disapproval exactly."

"Well, it isn't suspicion, is it? You don't think that Dorothy had any hand in the tragedy, do you?"

Carleton spoke savagely, with an abrupt change from his former manner, and as he heard his friend's words, Rob knew that he himself had no more suspicion of Dorthy Burt than he had of Carleton. She had testified in a constrained, uncertain manner, but that was not enough to rouse suspicion of her in any way.

"Of course not!" Fessenden declared heartily. "Don't be absurd. But have I your permission to put a few questions to Miss Burt, not in your presence?"

"Of course you have. I trust you to be kind and gentle with her, for she is a sensitive little thing; but I know whatever you may say to her, or she to you, will only make you see more clearly what a dear girl she is."

Fessenden was far from sure of this, but, having gained Carleton's permission to interview Miss Burt, he said no more about her just then.

For a long time the two men discussed the situation. But the more they talked the less they seemed able to form any plausible theory of the crime. At last Fessenden said, "There is one thing certain: if we are to believe Harris's statement about the locks and bolts, no one could have entered from the outside."

"No," said Carleton; "and so we're forced to turn our attention to some one inside the house. But each one in turn seems so utterly impossible. We cannot even suggest Mrs. Markham or Miss Morton——"

"I don't altogether like that Miss Morton. She acted queerly from the beginning."

"Not exactly queerly; she is not a woman of good breeding or good taste, but she only arrived that afternoon, and it's too absurd to picture her stabbing her hostess that night."

"I don't care how absurd it is; she profited by Miss Van Norman's death, and she was certainly avid to come into her inheritance at once."

"Yes, I know," said Schuyler almost impatiently. "But I saw Miss Morton when she first came downstairs, and though she was shocked, she really did nobly in controlling herself, and even in directing others what to do. You see, I was there, and I saw them all, and I'm sure that Miss Morton had no more to do with that dreadful deed than I had."

"Then what about her burning that will as soon as Miss Van Norman was dead?"

"I don't believe it was a will; and, in fact, I'm not sure she burned anything."

"Oh, yes, she did; I heard that French maid's story, when she first told it, and it was impossible to believe she was making it up. Besides, Miss French saw Miss Morton rummaging in the desk."

"She is erratic, I think, and perhaps, not over-refined; but I'm sure she never could have been the one to do that thing. Why, that woman is frightened at everything. She wouldn't dare commit a crime. She is fearfully timid."

"Dismissing Miss Morton, then, let us take the others, one by one. I think we may pass over Miss French and Miss Gardner. We have no reason to think of Mr. Hunt in this connection, and this brings us down to the servants."

"Not quite to the servants," said Carleton, with a peculiar look in his eyes that caught Rob's attention.

"Not quite to the servants? What do you mean?"

Carleton said nothing, but with a troubled gaze he looked intently at Fessenden.

"Cicely!" exclaimed Rob. "You think that?"

"I think nothing," said Carleton slowly, "and as an innocent man who was suspected, I hate to hint a suspicion of one who may be equally innocent. But does it not seem to you there are some questions to be answered concerning Miss Dupuy?"

Fessenden sat thinking for a long time. Surely these two men were just and even generous, and unwilling to suspect without cause.

"There are points to be explained," said Rob slowly; "and, Schuyler, since we are talking frankly, I must ask you this: do you know that Miss Dupuy is very much in love with you?"

"How absurd! That cannot be. Why, I've scarcely ever spoken to the girl."

"That doesn't matter—the fact remains. Now, you know she wrote that paper which stated that she loved S., but he did not love her. That initial designated yourself, and, because of this unfortunate attachment, Cicely was of course jealous, or rather envious, of Madeleine. I have had an interview with Miss Dupuy, in which she gave me much more information about herself than she thought she did, and one of the facts I discovered—from what she didn't say, rather than what she did—was her hopeless infatuation for you."

"It's difficult to believe this, but now that you tell me it is true, I can look back to some episodes which seem to indicate it. But I cannot think it would lead to such desperate results."

"There's one thing certain: when we do find the criminal it will have to be somebody we never would have dreamed of; for if there were any probable person we would suspect him already. Now, merely for the sake of argument, let us see if Cicely did not have 'exclusive opportunity' as well as yourself. Remember she was the last one who saw Miss Van Norman alive. I mean, so far as we have had any witness or evidence. This fact in itself is always a matter for investigation. And granting the fact of two women, both in love with you, one about to marry you, and the other perhaps insanely jealous; a weapon at hand, no one else astir in the house—is there not at least occasion for inquiry?"

Carleton looked aghast. He took up the story, and in a low voice said, "I can add to that. When I came in, as Hunt has testified, Cicely was leaning over the banister, still fully dressed. When I cried out for help fifteen minutes later, Cicely was the first to run downstairs. She asked no questions, she did not look toward the library, she glared straight at me with an indescribable expression of fear and horror. I cannot explain her attitude at that moment, but if this dreadful thing we have dared to think of could be true, it would perhaps be a reason."

"And then, you know, she tried to get possession secretly of that slip of paper, after it had served its purpose."

"Yes, and also after you, by clever observation, had discovered that she wrote it, and not Madeleine."

"Their writing is strangely alike."

"Yes; even I was deceived, and I have seen much of Madeleine's writing. Fessenden—this is an awful thing to hint—but do you suppose some of the notes I have had purporting to be from Miss Van Norman could have been written by Miss Dupuy?"

"Why not? Several people have said the secretary often wrote notes purporting to be from the mistress."

"Oh, yes; formal society notes. But I don't mean that. I mean, do you suppose Cicely could have written of her own accord—even unknown to Madeleine—as if—as if, you know, it were Madeleine herself writing?"

"Oh, on purpose to deceive you!"

"Yes, on purpose to deceive me. It could easily be done. I've seen so much of both their penmanship, and I never noticed it especially. I've always taken it for granted that a purely personal note was written by Madeleine herself. But now—I wonder."

"Do you mean notes of importance?"

"I mean notes that annoyed me. Notes that voluntarily referred to her going driving or walking with Willard, when there was no real reason for her referring to it. Could it be that Cicely—bah! I cannot say it of any woman!"

"I see your point; and it is more than possible that Miss Dupuy, knowing of the strained relations between you and Miss Van Norman, might have done anything she could to widen the breach. It would be easy, as she wrote so much of the correspondence, to do this unnoticed."

"Yes, that's what I mean. Often Madeleine's notes would contain a gratuitous bit of information about her and Willard, and though she frequently teased me when we were together, I was surprised at her writing these things. I feel sure now that sometimes, at least, they were the work of Miss Dupuy. I can't describe it exactly, but that would explain lots of things otherwise mysterious."

"This is getting beyond us," said Rob, with a quick sigh. "I think it my duty to report this to the coroner and to Detective Fairbanks, who is officially on the case. I thought I liked detective work, but I don't. It leads one toward too dreadful conclusions. Will you go with me, Carleton? I shall go at once to Mr. Benson."

"No, I think it would be better for you to go alone. Remember I am practically an accused man, and my word would be of little weight. Moreover, you are a lawyer, and it is your right and duty to make these things known. But unless forced to do so, I do not wish to testify against Miss Dupuy."

Remembering the girl's attitude toward Carleton, Rob could not wonder at this, and he went off alone to the coroner's.

XX

CICELY'S FLIGHT

Mr. Benson was astounded at the turn affairs had taken; but though it had seemed to him that all the evidence had pointed toward Carleton's guilt, he was really relieved to find another outlet for his suspicions. He listened attentively to what Fessenden said, and Rob was careful to express no opinion, but merely to state such facts as he knew in support of this new theory.

Detective Fairbanks was sent for, and he, too, listened eagerly to the latest developments.

It seemed to Rob that Mr. Fairbanks was rather pleased than otherwise to turn the trend of suspicion in another direction. And this was true, for though the detective felt a natural reluctance to suspect a woman, he had dreaded all along lest Carleton should be looked upon as a criminal merely because there was no one else to be considered. And Mr. Fairbanks's quick mind realized that if there were two suspects, there yet might be three, or more, and Schuyler Carleton would at least have a fair chance.

All things concerned seemed to have taken on a new interest, and Mr. Fairbanks proposed to begin investigations at once.

"But I don't see," he complained, "why Mr. Carleton so foolishly concealed that reliquary business. Why didn't he explain that at once?"

"Carleton is a peculiar nature," said Rob. "He is shrinkingly sensitive about his private affairs, and, being innocent, he had no fear at first that even suspicion would rest upon him, so he saw no reason to tell about what would have been looked upon as a silly superstition. Had he been brought to trial, he would doubtless have made a clean breast of the matter. He is a strange man, any way; very self-contained, abnormally sensitive, and not naturally frank. But if freed from suspicion he will be more approachable, and may yet be of help to us in our search."

"Of course, though," said Mr. Fairbanks thoughtfully, "you must realize that to a disinterested observer this affair of Mr. Carleton and Miss Burt does not help to turn suspicion away from him."

"I do realize that," said Rob; "but to an interested observer it looks different. Why, if Mr. Carleton were the guilty man, he surely would not tell me so frankly the story of his interest in Miss Burt."

This was certainly true, and Mr. Fairbanks agreed to it.

127

Rob had been obliged to tell the detective the facts of the case, though dilating as little as possible on Carleton's private affairs.

"At any rate," said Mr. Fairbanks, "we will not consider Mr. Carleton for the present, but turn toward the new trail, and it may lead us, at least, in the right direction. If Miss Dupuy is innocent, our investigations can do her no harm, and if she knows more than she has told, we may be able to learn something of importance. But she is of such a hysterical nature, it is difficult to hold a satisfactory conversation with her."

"Perhaps it would be advisable for me to talk to her first," said Rob. "I might put her more at her ease than a formidable detective could, and then I could report to you what I learn."

"Yes," agreed the other; "you could choose an expedient time, and, being in the same house, Miss French might help you."

"She could secure an interview for me quite casually, I am sure. And then, if I don't succeed, you can insist upon an official session, and question her definitely."

"There are indications," mused Mr. Fairbanks, "that accidental leaving of such a paper on the table is a little unlikely. If it were done purposely, it would be far easier to understand."

"Yes, and, granting there is any ground for suspicion, all Miss Dupuy's hysterics and disinclination to answer questions would be explained."

"Well, I hate to suspect a woman,—but we won't call it suspicion; we'll call it simply inquiry. You do what you can to get a friendly interview, and, if necessary, I'll insist on an official one later."

Rob Fessenden went straight over to the Van Norman house, eager to tell Kitty French the developments of the afternoon.

She was more than willing to revise her opinions, and was honestly glad that Mr. Carleton was practically exonerated.

"Of course there's nothing official," said Rob, after he had told his whole story, "but the burden of suspicion has been lifted from Carleton, wherever it may next be placed."

At first Kitty was disinclined to think Cicely could be implicated.

"She's such a slip of a girl!" she said. "I don't believe that little blue-eyed, yellow-haired thing could stab anybody."

"But you mustn't reason that way," argued Rob. "Opinions don't count at all. We must try to get at the facts. Now let us go at once and interview Miss Dupuy. Can't we see her in that sitting-room, as we did before? And she mustn't be allowed to faint this time."

"We can't help her fainting," declared Kitty, a little indignantly.

128

"You're just as selfish as all other men. Everything must bow to your will."

"I never pretended to any unmanly degree of unselfishness," said Rob blandly. "But we must have this interview at once. Will you go ahead and prepare the way?"

For answer Kitty ran upstairs and knocked at the door of what had been Madeleine's sitting-room, where Miss Dupuy was usually to be found at this hour of the day.

The door was opened by Marie, who replied to Kitty's question with a frightened air.

"Miss Dupuy? She is gone away. On the train, with luggage."

"Gone! Why, when did she go?"

"But a half-hour since. She went most suddenly."

"She did indeed! Does Miss Morton know of this?"

"That I do not know, but I think so."

Kitty turned to find Fessenden behind her, and as he had overheard the latter part of the conversation he came into the room and closed the door.

"Marie," he said to the maid, "tell us your idea of why Miss Dupuy went away."

"She was in fear," said Marie deliberately.

"In fear of what?"

"In fear of the detectives, and the questions they ask, and the dreadful coroner man. Miss Dupuy is not herself any more; she is so in fear she cannot sleep at night. Always she cries out in her dream."

Fessenden glanced at Kitty. "What does she say, Marie?" he asked.

"Nothing that I can understand, m'sieu; but always low cries of fear, and sometimes she murmurs, 'I must go away! I cannot again answer those dreadful questions. I shall betray my secret.' Over and over she mutters that."

Fessenden began to grow excited. Surely this was evidence, and Cicely's departure seemed to emphasize it. Without another word he went in search of Miss Morton.

"Did you know Miss Dupuy was going away?" he said abruptly to her.

"Yes," she replied. "The poor girl is completely worn out. For the last few days she has been looking over Madeleine's letters and papers and accounts, and she is really overworked, besides the fearful nervous strain we are all under."

"Where has she gone?"

"I don't know. I meant to ask her to leave an address, but she said she would write to me as soon as she reached her destination, and I thought no more about it."

129

"Miss Morton, she has run away. Some evidence has come to light that makes it seem possible she may be implicated in Madeleine's death, and her sudden departure points toward her guilt."

"Guilt! Miss Dupuy? Oh, impossible! She is a strange and emotional little creature, but she couldn't kill anybody. She isn't that sort."

"I'm getting a little tired of hearing that this one or that one 'isn't that sort.' Do you suppose anybody in decent society would ever be designated as one who is that sort? Unless the murderer was some outside tramp or burglar, it must have been some one probably not 'of that sort.' But, Miss Morton, we must find Miss Dupuy, and quickly. When did she go?"

"I don't know; some time ago, I think. I ordered the carriage to take her to the station. Perhaps she hasn't gone yet—from the station, I mean."

Rob looked at his watch. "Do you know anything about train times?" he asked.

"No except that there are not very many trains in the afternoon. I don't even know which way she is going."

Rob thought quickly. It seemed foolish to try to overtake the girl at the railway station, but it was the only chance. He dashed downstairs, and, catching up a cap as he rushed through the hall, he was out on the road in a few seconds, and running at a steady, practised gait toward the railroad. After he had gone a few blocks he saw a motor-car standing in front of a house. He jumped in and said to the astonished chauffeur, "Whiz me down to the railroad station, and I'll make it all right with your master, and with you, too."

The machine was a doctor's runabout, and the chauffeur knew that the doctor was making a long call, so he was not at all unwilling to obey this impetuous and masterful young man. Away they went, doubtless exceeding the speed limit, and in a short time brought up suddenly at the railroad station.

Rob jumped out, flung a bill to the chauffeur, gave him a card to give to his master, and waved a good-by as the motor-car vanished.

He strode into the station, only to be informed by the ticket-agent that a train had left for New York about a quarter of an hour since, and another would come along in about five minutes, which, though it made no regular stop at Mapleton, could be flagged if desired.

A few further questions brought out the information that a young woman corresponding to the description of Miss Dupuy had gone on that train.

Fessenden thought quickly. The second train, a fast one, he

130

knew would pass the other at a siding, and if he took it, he would reach New York before Cicely did, and could meet her there when she arrived at the station.

Had he had longer to consider, he might have acted differently, but on the impulse of the moment, he bought a ticket, said, "Flag her, please," and soon he was on the train actually in pursuit of the escaping girl.

As he settled himself in his seat, he rather enjoyed the fact that he was doing real detective work now. Surely Mr. Fairbanks would be pleased at his endeavors to secure the interview with Miss Dupuy under such difficulties.

But his plan to meet her at the Grand Central Station was frustrated by an unforeseen occurrence. His own train was delayed by a hot box, and he learned that he would not reach New York until after Miss Dupuy had arrived there.

Return from a way station was possible, but Rob didn't want to go back to Mapleton with his errand unaccomplished.

He thought it over, and decided on a radical course of action.

Instead of alighting there himself, he wrote a telegram which he had despatched from the way station to Miss Kitty French, and which ran:

> Gone to New York. Make M. tell C.'s address and wire
> me at the Waldorf.

It was a chance, but he took it and, any way, it meant only spending the night in New York, and returning to Mapleton next day, if his plan failed.

He had a strong conviction that Marie knew Cicely's address, although she had denied it. If this were true, Kitty could possibly learn it from her, and let him know in time to hunt up Cicely in New York. And if Marie really did not know the address, there was no harm done, after all.

The excitement of the chase stimulated Rob's mental activity, and he gave rein to his imagination.

If Cicely Dupuy were guilty, she would act exactly as she had done, he thought. A calmer, better-balanced woman would have stayed at Mapleton and braved it out, but Miss Dupuy's excitable temperament would not let her sleep or rest, and made it impossible for her to face inquiry discreetly.

Rob purposed, if he received the address he hoped for, to go to see the girl in New York, and by judicious kindliness of demeanor to learn more from her about the case than she would tell under legal pressure.

As it turned out, whatever might be his powers of detective acumen, his intuition regarding Marie's information was correct.

Kitty French, quickly catching the tenor of the telegram, took Marie aside, and commanded her to give up the address. Marie volubly protested and denied her knowledge, but Kitty was firm, and the stronger will conquered.

Luckily, Marie at last told, and Kitty went herself to send the telegram.

Marie accompanied her, as it was then well after dusk, but Kitty did not permit the girl to enter the telegraph office with her.

And so, by ten o'clock that evening, Rob Fessenden received from the hotel clerk a telegram bearing an address in West Sixty-sixth Street, which not only satisfied his wish, but caused him to feel greatly pleased at his own sagacity.

It was too late to go up there that evening, and so the amateur detective was forced to curb his impatience until the next morning. He was afraid the bird might have flown by that time, but there was no help for it. He thought of telephoning, but he didn't know the name of the people Cicely had gone to, and too, even if he could succeed in getting the call, such a proceeding would only startle her. So he devoted the rest of the evening to writing a letter to Kitty French, ostensibly to thank her for her assistance, but really for the pleasure of writing her. This he posted at midnight, thinking that if he should be detained longer than he anticipated, she would then understand why.

Next morning the eager young man ate his breakfast, and read his paper, a bit impatiently, while he waited for it to be late enough to start.

Soon after nine, he called a taxicab and went to the address Kitty had sent him.

Only the house number had been told in the message, so when Fessenden found himself in the vestibule of an apartment house, with sixteen names above corresponding bells, he was a bit taken aback.

"I wish I'd started earlier," he thought, "for it's a matter of trying them all until I strike the right one."

But he fancied he could deduce something from the names themselves, at least, for a start.

Eliminating one or two Irish sounding names, also a Smith and a Miller, he concluded to try first two names which were doubtless French.

The first gave him no success at all, but, undiscouraged, he tried the other.

"I wish to see Miss Dupuy," he said, to the woman who opened the door.

"She is not here," was the curt answer. But the intelligence in the woman's eye at the mention of the name proved to Fessenden that at least this was the place.

"Don't misunderstand," he said gently. "I want to see Miss Dupuy merely for a few moments' friendly conversation. It will be for her advantage to see me, rather than to refuse."

"But she is not here," repeated the woman. "There is no person of that name in my house."

"When did she go?" asked Rob quietly—so quietly that the woman was taken off her guard.

"About half an hour ago," she said, and then, with a horror-stricken look at her own thoughtlessness, she added hastily, "I mean my friend went. Your Miss Dupuy I do not know."

"Yes, you do," said Rob decidedly, "and as she has gone, you must tell me at once where she went."

The woman refused, and not until after a somewhat stormy scene, and some rather severe threats on Fessenden's part did she consent to tell that Cicely had gone to the Grand Central Station. More than this she would not say, and thinking he was wasting valuable time on her, Rob turned and, racing down the stairs, for there was no elevator, he jumped in his cab and whizzed away to the station.

133

XXI

A SUCCESSFUL PURSUIT

Before he entered the station he looked through the doorway, and to his delight saw the girl for whom he was looking.

He did not rush madly into the station, but paused a moment, and then walked in quietly, thinking that if his quest should be successful he must not frighten the excitable girl.

Cicely sat on one of the benches in the waiting-room. In her dainty travelling costume of black, and her small hat with its black veil, she looked so fair and young that Rob felt sudden misgivings as to his errand. But it must be done, and, quietly advancing, he took a seat beside her.

"Where are you going, Miss Dupuy?" he asked in a voice which was kinder and more gentle than he himself realized.

She looked up with a start, and said in a low voice, "Why do you follow me? May I not be left alone to go where I choose?"

"You may, Miss Dupuy, if you will tell me where you are going, and give me your word of honor that you will return if sent for."

"To be put through an examination! No, thank you. I'm going away where I hope I shall never see a detective or a coroner again!"

"Are you afraid of them, Miss Dupuy?"

The girl gave him a strange glance; but it showed anxiety rather than fear. However, her only reply was a low spoken "Yes."

"And why are you afraid?"

"I am afraid I may tell things that I don't want to tell." The girl spoke abstractedly and seemed to be thinking aloud rather than addressing her questioner.

It may be that Fessenden was influenced by her beauty or by the exquisite femininity of her dainty contour and apparel, but aside from all this he received a sudden impression that what this girl said did not betoken guilt. He could not have explained it to himself, but he was at the moment convinced that though she knew more than she had yet told, Cicely Dupuy was herself innocent.

"Miss Dupuy," he said very earnestly, "won't you look upon me as a friend instead of a foe? I am quite sure you can tell me more than you have told about the Van Norman tragedy. Am I wrong in thinking you are keeping something back?"

"I have nothing to tell," said Cicely, and the stubborn expression returned to her eyes.

It did not seem a very appropriate place in which to carry on such a personal conversation, but Fessenden thought perhaps the very publicity of the scene might tend to make Miss Dupuy preserve her equanimity better than in a private house. So he went on:

"Yes, you have several things to tell me, and I want you to tell me now. The last time I talked to you about this matter I asked you why you gave false evidence as to the time that Mr. Carleton entered the Van Norman house that evening, and you responded by fainting away. Now you must tell me why that question affected you so seriously."

"It didn't. I was nervous and overwrought, and I chanced to faint just then."

Fessenden saw that this explanation was untrue, but had been thought up and held ready for this occasion. He saw, too, that the girl held herself well in hand, so he dared to be more definite in his inquiries.

"Do you know, Miss Dupuy, that you are seriously incriminating yourself when you give false evidence?"

"I don't care," was the answer, not flippantly given, but with an earnestness of which the speaker herself seemed unaware.

And Fessenden was a good enough reader of character to perceive that she spoke truthfully.

The only construction he could put upon this was that, as he couldn't help believing, the girl was innocent and therefore feared no incriminating evidence against her.

But in that case what was she afraid of, and why was she running away?

"Miss Dupuy," he began, starting on a new tack, "please show more confidence in me. Will you answer me more straightforwardly if I assure you of my belief in your own innocence? I will not conceal from you the fact that not every one is so convinced of that as I am, and so I look to you for help to establish it."

"Establish what? My innocence?" said Cicely, and now she looked bewildered, rather than afraid. "Does anybody think that I killed Miss Van Norman?"

"Without going so far as to say any one thinks so, I will tell you that they think there are indications that point to such a thing."

"How absurd!" said Cicely, and the honesty of her tone seemed to verify Fessenden's conviction that whatever guilty knowledge this girl might possess, she herself was innocent of crime.

"If it is an absurd idea, then why not return to Mapleton and answer any queries that may be put to you? You are innocent, therefore you have nothing to fear."

"I have a great deal to fear."

The girl spoke gently, even sadly, now. She seemed full of

135

anxiety and sorrow, that yet showed no trace of apprehension for herself.

All at once a light broke upon Fessenden. She was shielding somebody. Nor was it hard to guess who it might be!

"Miss Dupuy," began Rob again, eagerly this time, "I have succeeded in establishing, practically, Mr. Carleton's innocence. May I not likewise establish your own?"

"Mr. Carleton's innocence!" repeated the girl, clasping her hands. "Oh, is that true? Then who did do it?"

"We don't know yet," went on Rob, hastening to make the most of the advantage he had gained; "but having assured you that it was not Schuyler Carleton, will you not tell me what it is you have been keeping secret?"

"How do you know Mr. Carleton is innocent? Have you proved it? Has some one else confessed?"

"No, no one has confessed. And, indeed, I may as well own up that no one is quite so sure of Mr. Carleton's innocence as I am myself. But I am sure of it, and I'm going to prove it. Now, will you not help me to do so?"

"How can I help you?"

"By explaining that discrepancy in time, so far as you can. You testified that Mr. Carleton entered the house at half-past eleven, and Mr. Hunt said he came in at quarter-past. What made you tell that falsehood, and stick to it?"

"Why, nothing," exclaimed Cicely, "except that I thought I saw Mr. Carleton come into the house some little time before he cried out for help. I was looking over the baluster when Mr. Hunt said he saw me, and I, too, thought it was Mr. Carleton who came in then."

"It was Mr. Carleton, but he has satisfactorily explained why he came in, and what he was doing until the time when he called out for help. Why did you not tell us about this at first?"

"I was afraid—afraid they might connect Mr. Carleton with the murder, and I was afraid——"

"You were afraid that he really had done the deed?"

"Yes," said Cicely in a very low voice, but with an intonation that left no doubt of her truthfulness.

"Then," said Rob in his kindest way, "you may set your mind at rest. Mr. Carleton is no longer under actual suspicion, and you may go away, as you intended, for a few days' rest. I should be glad to have your address, though I trust it will not be necessary for me to send for you; and I know you will not be called to witness against Schuyler Carleton."

Cicely gave the required address, and though they continued the conversation for a short time, Rob concluded that the girl knew

136

nothing that actually bore on the case. Her own false evidence and nervous apprehension had all been because of her anxiety about Mr. Carleton, and her fear that he had really been the murderer. Her written paper, and all the evidences of her jealousy of Miss Van Norman, were the result of her secret and unrequited love for the man, and her attempted flight was only because she feared that her uncontrollable emotion and impulsive utterances might help to incriminate him.

Fessenden was truly sorry for her, and glad that she could go away from the trying scenes for a time. He felt sure that she would come, if summoned, for now, relieved of her doubt of Carleton, she had no reason for refusing any testimony she could give.

It was in a kindly spirit that he bade her good-by, and promised to use every effort not only to establish Carleton's innocence, but to discover the guilty one.

When Fessenden returned to the Van Norman house, several people were awaiting him in the library. Miss Morton and Kitty French were there, also Coroner Benson and Detective Fairbanks.

"Were you too late?" asked Kitty, as Rob entered the room.

"No, not too late. I found Miss Dupuy in the Grand Central station, and I had a talk with her."

"Well?" said Kitty impatiently.

"She is as innocent as you or I."

"How did you find it out so quickly?" inquired Mr. Fairbanks, who had a real liking for the enthusiastic young fellow.

"Why, I found out that she was hanging over the baluster, as Hunt said; and she did see Carleton come in at quarter after eleven. She then went back to her room, and heard Carleton cry out at half-past eleven, and when she discovered what had happened she suspected Carleton of the deed; and, endeavoring to shield him, she refused to give evidence that might incriminate him."

"But," cried Kitty, "of course Mr. Carleton didn't do it if Cicely did."

"But don't you see, Miss French," said the older detective, as Fessenden sat staring in blank surprise at what he deemed Kitty's stupidity—"don't you see that if Miss Dupuy suspected Mr. Carleton she couldn't by any possibility be guilty herself."

"Why, of course she couldn't!" exclaimed Kitty. "And I'm truly glad, for I can't help liking that girl, if she is queer. But, then, who did do it?"

Suspicion was again at a standstill. There was no evidence to point anywhere; there were no clues to follow, and no one had any suggestion to offer.

It was at this juncture that Tom Willard and Schuyler Carleton came in together.

They were told of Fessenden's interview with Miss Dupuy at the station, and Carleton expressed himself as thoroughly glad that the girl was exonerated. He said little, however, for it was a delicate subject, since it all hinged on Miss Dupuy's affection for himself.

Tom Willard listened to Fessenden's recital, but he only said that nothing would ever have induced him to suspect Miss Dupuy, any way, for it could not have been the deed of a fragile young girl.

"The blow that killed Maddy was powerfully dealt," said Tom; "and I can't help thinking it was some tramp or professional burglar who was clever enough to elude Harris's fastenings. Or some window may have been overlooked that night. At any rate, we have no more plausible theory."

"We have not," said Mr. Fairbanks; "but I for one am not content to let the matter rest here. I should like to suggest that we call in some celebrated detective, whose experience and skill would discover what is beyond the powers of Mr. Fessenden and myself."

Rob felt flattered that Mr. Fairbanks classed him with himself, and felt anxious too that the suggestion of employing a more skilful detective should be carried out.

"But," objected Coroner Benson, "to engage a detective of high standing would entail considerable expense, and I'm not sure that I'm authorized to sanction this."

There was a silence, but nearly every one in the room was thinking that surely this was the time for Tom Willard to make use of his lately inherited Van Norman money.

Nor was Willard delinquent. Though showing no overwillingness in the matter, he said plainly that he would be glad if Coroner Benson or Mr. Fairbanks would engage the services of the best detective they could find, and allow him to defray all expenses attendant thereon.

At this a murmur of approval went round the room. All his hearers were at their wits' end what to do next, and the opportunity of putting a really great detective on the case was welcome indeed.

"But I don't believe," said Willard, "that he will find out anything more than our own men have discovered." The appreciative glance Tom gave Mr. Fairbanks and Rob quite soothed whatever touch of jealousy they may have felt of the new detective.

It was Carleton who suggested Fleming Stone. He did not know the man personally, but he had read and heard of the wonderful work he had done in celebrated cases all over the country.

Of course they had all heard of Fleming Stone, and each felt a thrill of gratitude to Willard, whose wealth made it possible to employ the great detective.

Mr. Fairbanks wasted no time, but wrote at once to Fleming Stone, and received a reply stating that he would arrive in Mapleton in a few days.

But in the meantime Rob Fessenden could not be idle.

In truth, he had a secret ambition to solve the mystery himself, before the great detective came, and to this end he stayed on in Mapleton, and racked his brain for ideas on the subject.

Mr. Fairbanks was more easily discouraged, and frankly confessed the case was beyond his powers.

Privately, he still suspected Mr. Carleton, but in the face of Rob's faith in his friend, and also because of the demeanor of Carleton himself, he couldn't avow his suspicions.

For since Fessenden's assertions of confidence, Carleton had changed in his attitude toward the world at large.

Still broken and saddened by the tragedy, he did not show that abject and self-condemnatory air which had hung round him during the inquest week.

Kitty French had almost recovered faith in him, and had there been any one else at all to suspect, she would have asserted her belief in his innocence.

Carleton himself seemed baffled. His suspicions had been directed toward Cicely, because he could see no other possibility; but the proof of her suspicions of himself, of course, showed he was wrong in the matter.

He could suggest nothing; he could think of nobody who might have done the deed, and he was thoroughly content to place the whole affair unreservedly in the hands of Fleming Stone.

Indeed, every one seemed to be glad of the expected help, if we except Fessenden. He was restlessly eager to do something himself, and saw no reason why he shouldn't keep on trying until Stone came.

XXII

A TALK WITH MISS MORTON

Of course Fessenden confided his wishes to Kitty French. Equally of course, that obliging young woman was desirous of helping him attain them. But neither of them could think of new lines of investigation to pursue.

"We've no clue but that little cachou," said Miss French, by way of summing up; "and as that's no good at all, we have really nothing that can be called a clue."

"No," agreed Rob, "and we have no suspect. Now that Carleton and Miss Dupuy are both out of it, I don't see who could have done it."

"I never felt fully satisfied about Miss Morton and her burned paper," said Kitty thoughtfully.

They were walking along a village road while carrying on this conversation, so there was no danger of Miss Morton's overhearing them.

"I've never felt satisfied about that woman, any way," said Rob. "The oftener I see her the less I like her. She's too smug and complacent. And yet when she was questioned, she went all to pieces."

"Well, as she flatly contradicted what Marie had said, of course they couldn't keep on questioning her. You can't take a servant's word against a lady's."

"You ought to, in a serious case like this. I say, Kitty, let's go there now and have a heart-to-heart talk with her."

Kitty laughed at the idea of a heart-to-heart talk between those two people, but said she was willing to go.

"It mayn't amount to anything," went on Rob, "and yet, it may. I've asked Mr. Fairbanks to chase up that burned paper matter, but he said there was nothing in it. He didn't hear Marie's story, you see,—he only heard it retold, and he doesn't know how sincere that girl seemed to be when she told about it."

"Yes, and I saw Miss Morton in Maddy's room, too. I think she ought to tell what she was up to."

So to the Van Norman house went the two inquisitors, and had Miss Morton known of their fell designs she might not have greeted them as cordially as she did.

Miss Morton had grown fond of Kitty French during the girl's

140

stay with her, and she looked with approval on the fast-growing friendship between her and young Fessenden.

As the hostess at the Van Norman house, too, Miss Morton showed a kindly hospitality, and though she was without doubt eccentric, and sometimes curt of speech, she conducted the household and directed the servants with very little friction or awkwardness.

She was most friendly toward Tom Willard and Schuyler Carleton, and the latter often dropped in at the tea hour. Fessenden dropped in at any hour of the day, and of course Mr. Fairbanks came and went as he chose.

Fessenden and Kitty found Miss Morton in the library, and, as they had decided beforehand, went straight to the root of the matter.

"Miss Morton," Fessenden began, "I want to do a little more questioning on my own account, before Mr. Fleming Stone arrives. I'm sure you won't object to helping me out a bit by answering a few queries."

"Go ahead," said Miss Morton grimly, but not unkindly.

"They are a bit personal," went on Rob, who was at a loss how to begin, now that he was really told to do so.

"Well?"

This time, Miss Morton's tone was more crisp, and Kitty began to see that Rob was on the wrong tack. So she took the helm herself, and said, with a winning smile:

"We want you to tell us frankly what was the paper you burned."

Something in Miss Morton's expression went to the girl's heart, and she added impulsively:

"I know it wasn't anything that affects the case at all, and if you want to refuse us, you may."

"I'd rather not tell you," said Miss Morton, and a far-away look came into her strange eyes; "but since you have shown confidence in me, I prefer to return it."

She took Kitty's hand in hers, and from the gentle touch the girl was sure that whatever was the nature of the coming confidence, it was not that of a guilty conscience.

"As you know, Kitty," she began, addressing the girl, though she glanced at Rob occasionally, "many years ago I was betrothed to Richard Van Norman. We foolishly allowed a trifling quarrel to separate us for life. I will not tell you the story of that now,—though I will, some time, if you care to hear it. But we were both quick-tempered, and the letters that passed between us at that time were full of hot, angry, unconsidered words. They were letters such as no

141

human beings ought to have written to each other. Perhaps it was because of their exceeding bitterness, which we read and reread, that we never made up that quarrel, though neither of us ever loved any one else, or ceased to love the other. At the death of Richard Van Norman, two years or more ago, I burned his letters which I had kept so long, and I wrote to Madeleine, asking her to return mine to me if they should be found among her uncle's papers."

"Dear Miss Morton," said Kitty, "don't tell any more if it pains you. We withdraw our request, don't we, Rob?"

"Yes, indeed," said Fessenden heartily; "forgive us, Miss Morton, for what is really an intrusion, and an unwarrantable one."

"I want to tell you a little more," Miss Morton resumed, "and afterward I'll tell you why I've told it. Madeleine replied with a most kind letter, saying she had not found the letters, but should she ever do so, she would send them to me. About a year ago, she wrote and asked me to come here to see her. I came, thinking she had found those letters. She had not, but she had found her uncle's diary, which disclosed his feelings toward me, both before and after our quarrel, and she told me then she intended to leave this place to me in her will, because she thought it ought to be mine. Truth to tell, I didn't take much interest in this bequest, for I supposed the girl would long outlive me. But I had really no desire for the house without its master, and though I didn't tell her so, I would rather have had the letters which I hoped she had found, than the news of her bequest."

"Why did you want the letters so much, Miss Morton?" asked Kitty.

"Because, my dear, they were a disgrace to me. They would be a disgrace to any woman alive. You, my child, with your gentle disposition, can't understand what dreadful cruelty an angry woman can be guilty of on paper. Well, again Madeleine told me she would give me the letters if they ever appeared, and I went home. I didn't hear from her again till shortly before her wedding, when she wrote me that the letters had been found in a secret drawer of Richard's old desk. She invited me to come to her wedding, and said that she would then give me the letters. Of course I came, and that afternoon that I arrived she told me they were in her desk, and she would give them to me next morning. I was more than impatient for them,—I had waited forty years for them,—but I couldn't trouble her on her wedding eve. And then—when—when she went away from us, without having given them into my possession, I was so afraid they would fall into other hands, that I went in search of them. I found them in her desk, I took them to my room and burned them without reading them. And that is the true story of the burned papers. I did look over a memorandum book, thinking it might tell where they were. But right after that I found the letters themselves in the next compartment, and I took them. They were mine."

The dignified complacency with which Miss Morton uttered that last short sentence commanded the respect of her hearers.

"Indeed, they were yours, Miss Morton," said Fessenden, "and I'm glad you secured them, before other eyes saw them."

Kitty said nothing, but held Miss Morton's hand in a firm, gentle pressure that seemed to seal their friendship.

"But," said Fessenden, a little diffidently, "why didn't you tell all this at the inquest as frankly as you have told us?"

Miss Morton paled, and then grew red.

"I am an idiot about such things," she said. "When questioned publicly, like that, I am so embarrassed and also so fearful that I scarcely know what I say. I try to hide this by a curt manner and a bravado of speech, with the result that I get desperate and say anything that comes into my head, whether it's the truth or not. I not only told untruths, but I contradicted myself, when witnessing, but I couldn't seem to help it. I lost control of my reasoning powers, and finally I felt my only safety was in denying it all. For—and this was my greatest fear—I thought they might suspect that I killed Madeleine, if they knew I did burn the papers. Afterward, I would have confessed that I had testified wrongly, but I couldn't see how it would do any good."

"No," said Rob slowly, "except to exonerate Marie of falsehood."

Miss Morton set her lips together tightly, and seemed unwilling to pursue that subject.

"And now," she said, "the reason I've told you two young people this, is because I want to warn you not to let a quarrel or a foolish misunderstanding of any sort come between you to spoil the happiness that I see is in store for you."

"Good for you! Miss Morton!" cried Rob. "You're a brick! You've precipitated matters a little; Kitty and I haven't put it into words as yet, but—we accept these preliminary congratulations,—don't we, dear?"

And foolish little Kitty only smiled, and buried her face on Miss Morton's shoulder instead of the young man's!

And so, Miss Morton's name was erased from Rob's list of people to be inquired of, and, as he acknowledged to himself, he was quite ready now to turn over his share in the case to Fleming Stone.

And, too, since Miss Morton had given a gentle push to the rolling stone of his affair with Kitty, it rolled faster, and the two young people had their heart-to-heart talks with each other, instead of adding a third to the interview.

143

But there was just one more unfinished duty that Fessenden determined to attend to. Carleton had assured him that he was at liberty to talk to Dorothy Burt, if he chose, and Rob couldn't help thinking that he ought to get all possible light on the case before Mr. Stone came; for he proposed to assist that gentleman greatly by his carefully tabulated statements, and his cross-referenced columns of evidence.

So, unaccompanied by Kitty, who was apt to prove a disturbing influence on his concentration of mind, he interviewed Miss Burt.

It was not difficult to get an opportunity, as she rarely left the house, and Mrs. Carleton was not exigent in her demands on her companion's time.

So the two strolled in the rose-garden late one afternoon, and Rob asked Miss Burt to tell him why she hesitated so when on the witness stand, and why she looked at Carleton with such unmistakable glances of inquiry, which he as certainly answered.

Dorothy Burt replied to the questions as frankly as they were put.

"To explain it to you, Mr. Fessenden," she said, "I must first tell you that I loved Mr. Carleton even while Miss Van Norman was his affianced bride. I tell you this simply, both because it is the simple truth and because Mr. Carleton advised me to tell you, if you should ask me. And, knowing this, you may be surprised to learn that when I heard of Miss Van Norman's death, I——" she raised her wonderful eyes and looked straight at Rob—"I thought she died by Schuyler's hand. Yes, you may well look at me in surprise,—I know it was dreadful of me to think he could have done it, but—I did think so. You see, I loved him,—and I knew he loved me. He had never told me so, had never breathed a word that was disloyal to Miss Van Norman,—and yet I knew. And that last evening in this very rose-garden, on the night before his wedding, we walked here together, and I knew from what he didn't say, not from what he did say, that it was I whom he loved, and not she. He left me with a few cold, curt words that I knew only too well masked his real feelings, and I saw him no more that night. He had told me he was going over to Miss Van Norman's, and so, when I heard of the—the tragedy—I couldn't help thinking he had yielded to a sudden terrible impulse. Oh, I'm not defending myself for my wrong thought of him; I'm only confessing that I did think that."

"And how did you learn that you were mistaken," said Rob gently, "and that Schuyler didn't do it?"

"Why, the very next night he told me he loved me," said the girl, her face alight with a tender glory, "and then I knew!"

144

"And your embarrassment at the questions on the witness stand?"

"Was only because I knew suspicion was directed toward him, and I feared I might say something to strengthen it, even while trying to do the opposite."

"And you didn't care whether you told the truth or not?"

"If the truth would help to incriminate Schuyler, I would prefer not to tell it."

The gentle sadness in Dorothy's tone robbed this speech of the jarring note it would otherwise have held.

"You are right, Miss Burt," said Rob, "and I thank you for the frank confidence you have shown in talking to me as freely as you have done."

"Schuyler told me to," said the girl simply.

XXIII

FLEMING STONE

When Fessenden told Kitty of his interview with Dorothy Burt, she agreed that he had now followed every trail that had presented itself, or had been suggested by anybody.

Mr. Fairbanks, too, admitted that he was at his wits' end, and saw no hope of a solution of the mystery except through the services of Fleming Stone. And so when the great detective arrived, both Fairbanks and Fessenden were ready to do anything they could to help him, but had no suggestions to make.

With her ever-ready hospitality, Miss Morton invited Mr. Stone to make his home at the Van Norman house, and, as this quite coincided with his own wishes, Stone took up his quarters there.

The first evening of his arrival he listened to the details of the case.

Fleming Stone was of a most attractive personality. He was nearly fifty years old, with graying hair and a kindly, responsive face.

At dinner he had won the admiration of all by his tact and interesting conversation. At the table the business upon which he had come had not been mentioned, but now the group assembled in the library felt that the time had come to talk of the matter.

It was a strangely-assorted household. Tom Willard, though the only relative of the Van Normans present, was in no way the head of the house. That position was held by Miss Morton, who, though kind-hearted and hospitable, never let it be forgotten that she was owner and mistress of the mansion.

Kitty French was an honored guest, and as Miss Morton had invited her to stay as long as she would, she had determined now to stay through Mr. Stone's sojourn there, after which, whatever the results of his work, she would go back to her home in New York.

Fessenden and Schuyler Carleton had been with them at dinner, and Mr. Benson and Mr. Fairbanks had come later, and now the group waited only on Mr. Stone's pleasure to begin the recital of the case.

When Fleming Stone, then, asked Coroner Benson to give him the main facts, it seemed as if the great detective's work was really about to begin.

"Would you rather see Mr. Benson alone?" asked Schuyler

Carleton, actuated, doubtless, by his own shrinking from any publicity.

"Not at all," said Stone briefly. "I prefer that you all should feel free to speak whenever you wish."

Then Mr. Benson set forth in a concise way and in chronological order the facts as far as they were known, the suspicions that had been entertained and given up; and deplored the entire lack of clue or evidence that might lead to investigation in any definite direction.

The others, as Mr. Stone had suggested, made remarks when they chose, and the whole conversation was of an informal and colloquial nature. It seemed dominated by Fleming Stone's mind. He drew opinions from one or another, until before they realized it every one present had taken part in the recital. And to each Fleming Stone listened with deference and courtesy. The coroner's legal phrases, Fessenden's impetuous suggestions, Tom's blunt remarks, Carleton's half-timid utterances, Kitty's volatile sallies, and even Miss Morton's futile observations, all were listened to and responded to by Fleming Stone with an air of deep interest and consideration.

As the hour grew late Mr. Stone said that he felt thoroughly acquainted with the facts of the case so far as they could be told to him. He said he could express no opinion nor offer any suggestion that night, but that he hoped to come to some conclusions on the following day; and if they would all meet him in the same place the next evening, he would willingly disclose whatever he might have learned or discovered in the meantime. This put an end to the conversation, and Mr. Benson and Mr. Fairbanks went home. The ladies went to their rooms, and Carleton, Fessenden and Willard sat up for an hour's smoke with Fleming Stone, who entertained them with talk on subjects far removed from murder or sudden death.

The next morning Fleming Stone expressed a desire to be shown all the rooms in the house.

"In a case like this," he said, "with no definite clues to follow, the only thing to do is to examine the premises in hope of happening upon something suggestive."

Kitty was eager to be Mr. Stone's guide, and easily obtained Miss Morton's permission to go into all the rooms of the old mansion.

Fessenden went with them, and though the tour of the sleeping-rooms was quickly made, it was evident that the quick eye of the detective took in every detail that was visible. He stayed longer in Madeleine's sitting-room, but, though he picked up a few papers

147

from her desk and glanced at them, he showed no special interest in the room.

Downstairs they went then, and found Mr. Fairbanks in the library, awaiting them. He brought no news or fresh evidence, and had merely called in hope of seeing Mr. Stone.

The great detective was most frank and kindly toward his lesser colleague, and made him welcome with a genial courtesy.

"I'm going to make a thorough examination of these lower rooms," said Fleming Stone, "and I should be glad of the assistance of you two younger men. My eyes are not what they once were."

Mr. Fairbanks and Rob well knew that this statement was merely an idle compliment to themselves; for the eyes of Fleming Stone had never yet missed a clue, however obscurely hidden.

But Kitty, ignorant of the principles of professional etiquette, really thought that Fleming Stone was depending on his two companions for assistance.

Tom Willard had gone out, and Miss Morton was looking after her all-important housekeeping, so the three men and Kitty French were alone in the library.

In his quick, quiet way Fleming Stone went rapidly round the room. He examined the window fixtures and curtains, the mantel and fireplace, the furniture and carpet, and came to a standstill by the library table. The dagger, which was kept in a drawer of the table, was shown to him, but though he examined it a moment, it seemed to have little interest for him.

"There's not a clue in this room," he said almost indignantly. "There probably were several the morning after the murder, but the thorough sweepings and dustings since have obliterated every trace."

Somewhat abruptly he went into the large hall. Here his proceedings in the library were duplicated. "Nothing at all," he said; "but what could be expected in a room which is a general thoroughfare?"

Then he went into the drawing-room. The other three followed, feeling rather depressed at the hopeless outlook, and a little disappointed in the great detective.

Stone glanced around the large apartment.

"Swept, scrubbed, and polished," he declared, as he glanced with disfavor at the immaculate room.

"And indeed it was quite necessary," said Miss Morton, who entered just then. "After all those vines and flowers were taken away, and as a good deal of the furniture was out, I took occasion for a good bit of house-cleaning."

148

"Well," said Fleming Stone quietly, "there's one clue they didn't sweep away. Here is where the assassin entered."

As he spoke Mr. Stone was leaning against the mantel and looking down at the immaculately brushed hearth.

"Where?" cried Kitty, darting forward, and though the others gave no voice to their curiosity, they waited breathlessly for Stone's next utterance.

The hearth and the whole fireplace were tiled, and in the floor tiling, under the andirons, was a rectangular iron plate with an oval opening closed by an iron cover. This cover was hinged, and could be raised and thrown back to permit ashes to be swept into the chute. The iron plate was sunk flush with the hearth and cemented into the brick-work, and the cover fitted into the rim so closely that scarce a seam showed.

"He came up through this hole in the fireplace," said Stone, almost as if talking to himself, "very soon after Miss Dupuy went upstairs at half-past ten. Before Mr. Carleton arrived at quarter after eleven, the murderer had finished his work, and had departed by this same means."

While the others stood seemingly struck dumb by this revelation, Kitty excitedly flew to the fireplace and tried to raise the iron lid, but the andirons were in the way. Rob set them aside for her, while Stone said quietly, "Those andirons were probably not there that night?"

"No," exclaimed Kitty; "they had been taken away, because we expected to fill the fireplace with flowers the next day."

"But how could anybody get in the cellar?" asked Miss Morton, looking bewildered.

"The cellar is never carefully locked," said Fleming Stone. "I came downstairs early this morning, and before breakfast Harris had shown me all through the cellar. He admits that several windows are always left open for the sake of ventilation, and claims that the carefully locked door in the hall at the head of the cellar stairs precludes all danger from that direction."

"But I don't understand," said Mr. Fairbanks perplexedly. "If that opening is an ash-chute, such as I have in my own house, it is all bricked up down below, with the exception of a small opening for the removal of the ashes, and it would be quite impossible for any one to climb up through it."

"But this one isn't bricked up," said Fleming Stone. "It was originally intended to be enclosed; but it seems this fireplace is rarely used. Harris tells me that the late Mr. Van Norman used to talk about having the chute completed, and having a fire here more often. But the library wood fire was more attractive as a family gathering place, and this formal room was used only on state occasions. However, as you see," and Mr. Stone raised the iron lid again, "this opens directly into the cellar, and, I repeat, formed the means of entrance for the murderer of Madeleine Van Norman."

Fleming Stone's voice and manner were far from triumphant or jubilant at his discovery. He seemed rather to state the fact with regret, but as if it must be told.

Mr. Fairbanks looked amazed and thoughtful, but Rob Fessenden was frankly incredulous.

"Mr. Stone," he said respectfully, "I am sure you know what you're talking about, but will you tell me how a man could get up through that hole? It doesn't seem to me that a small-sized boy could squeeze through."

Fleming Stone took a silver-cased tape-measure from his pocket, and handed it to Rob without a word.

Eagerly stooping on the hearth, Rob measured the oval opening in the iron plate. Although the rectangular plate was several inches larger each way, the oval opening measured exactly nine and one-half inches by thirteen and one-half inches.

"Who could get through that?" he inquired, as he announced the figures. "I'm sure I couldn't."

"And Schuyler Carleton is a larger man than you are," observed Mr. Fairbanks.

"That lets Tom Willard out, too," said Rob, with a slight smile; "for he's nearly six feet tall, and weighs more than two hundred pounds."

"The only man I know of," said Mr. Fairbanks thoughtfully, "who could come up through that hole is Slim Jim."

"Who is Slim Jim?" cried Rob quickly. "Go for him; he is the man!"

"Not so fast," said Mr. Fairbanks. "Slim Jim is a noted burglar and a suspected murderer, but he is safely in prison at present and has been for some months."

"But he may have escaped," exclaimed Rob. "Are you sure he hasn't?"

"I haven't heard anything about him of late; but if he is or has been away from the prison, it can be easily found out."

"Isn't it unlikely," said Fleming Stone quietly, "that a noted burglar should enter a house and commit murder, without making any attempt to steal?"

"He may have been frightened away by the sound of Schuyler's latch-key," suggested Rob, and Kitty looked at him with pride in his ingenuity, and thought how much cleverer he was, after all, than the celebrated Fleming Stone.

150

Fessenden urged Mr. Fairbanks to go at once and look up the whereabouts of Slim Jim, and the detective was strongly inclined to go.

"Go, by all means, if you choose," said Fleming Stone pleasantly. "There's really nothing further to do here in the way of examination of the premises. I do not mind saying that my own suspicions are not directed toward Slim Jim, but my own suspicions are by no means an infallible guide. I will ask you, though, gentlemen, not to say anything about this ash-chute matter to-day. I consider it is my right to request this. Of course you can find out all about Slim Jim without stating how he entered the house."

The two men promised not to say anything about the ash-chute to anybody, and hot upon the trail of the suspected burglar they went away.

Miss Morton excused herself, and upon Kitty French fell the burden of entertaining Mr. Stone. Nor was this young woman dismayed at the task.

Though not loquacious, the detective was an easy and pleasant talker, and he seemed quite ready to converse with the girl as if he had no other occupation on hand.

"How wonderful you are!" said Kitty, clasping her hands beneath her chin as she looked at the great man. "To think of your spotting that fireplace thing right away! Though of course I never should have thought of anybody squeezing up through there. And Rob and I spent a whole morning searching these rooms for clues, and that was only the day after it happened."

"What an opportunity!" Stone seemed interested. "And didn't you find anything—not anything?"

"No, not a thing. We were so disappointed. Oh, yes, Rob did find one little thing, but it was so little and so silly that I guess he forgot all about it."

"What was it?"

"Why, I've almost forgotten the name. Oh, yes, Rob said it was a cachou—a little silver thing, you know, like a tiny pill. Rob says some men eat them after they've been smoking. But he asked all the men that ever came here, and they all said they didn't use them. Maybe the burglar dropped it."

"Maybe he did. Where did you find it?"

"Rob found it. It was right in that corner by the mantel, just near the fireplace."

Fleming Stone stood up. "Miss French," said he, "if it is any satisfaction to you, you may know that you have helped me a great deal in my work. Will you excuse me now, as I find I have important business elsewhere?"

Kitty smiled and bowed politely, but after Mr. Stone had left her she wondered what she could have said or done that helped him; and she wondered, too, what had caused that unspeakably sad look in his eyes as he went away.

XXIV

A CONFESSION

Mr. Taylor, the landlord of the Mapleton Inn, showed a pleased surprise when Fleming Stone walked into his hotel and approached the desk. The men had never met, but everybody in Mapleton knew that Fleming Stone was in town, and had heard repeated and accurate descriptions of his appearance.

"Perhaps you can spare half an hour for a smoke and a chat," said Stone affably, and though Mr. Taylor heartily agreed, he did not confess that he could easily have spared half a day or more had the great detective asked him.

In the landlord's private office they sat down for a smoke, and soon the conversation, without effort, drifted around to the Van Norman affair.

Unlike detectives of fiction, Fleming Stone was by no means secretive or close-mouthed. Indeed he was discursive, and Mr. Taylor marvelled that such a great man should indulge in such trivial gossip. They talked of old Richard Van Norman and the earlier days of the Van Norman family.

"You've lived here a long time, then?" inquired Mr. Stone.

"Yes, sir. Boy and man, I've lived here nigh onto sixty years."

"But this fine modern hotel of yours is not as old as that?"

The landlord's face glowed with pride. "Right you are, sir. Some few years ago wife had some money left her, and we built the old place over—pretty near made a whole new house of it."

"You have many guests?"

"Well, not as many as I'd like; but as many as I can expect in a little town like this. Mostly transients, of course; drummers and men of that sort. Young Willard stayed here, when the Van Norman house was full of company, but after the—the trouble, he went back there to stay."

"Affable sort of man, Willard, isn't he?" observed Stone.

"Yes, he's all of that, but he's a scapegrace. He used to lead this town a dance when he lived here."

"How long since he lived here?"

"Oh, he's only been away a matter of three years, or that. 'Bout a year before his uncle died they quarrelled. They both had the devil's own temper, and they had quarrelled before, but this time it was for keeps; and so off goes Mr. Tom, and never turns up again until he comes to Miss Madeleine's wedding."

"Was he in any business when he lived here?"

"Yes, he had a good position as engineer in a big factory. He was a good worker, Tom was, and not afraid of anything. Always jolly and good-natured, except when he'd have one of them fearful fits of temper. Then he was like a raging lion—no, more like a tiger; quiet-like, but deep and desperate."

Soon after Fleming Stone rose to go. "Thank you very much," he said politely, "for your half-hour. And, by the way, have you any cachous? I find I haven't any with me, and after smoking, you know, before going back to the ladies——"

"Yes, yes, I know; but I don't happen to have any. But wait a minute, I believe Tripp has some."

He threw open the door and gave a quick whistle.

A boy appeared so suddenly that he could not have been far away, and, moreover, his sharp black eyes and alert manner betokened the type of boy who would be apt to be listening about.

His hand was already in his pocket when Mr. Taylor said to him, "Tripp, didn't I see you have a small bottle of cachous?—those little silver pellets, you know."

"Yessir;" and Tripp drew forth a half-filled bottle.

"That's right. Give them to the gentleman."

"Oh, I only want a couple," said Fleming Stone, taking the vial which Tripp thrust toward him. "Where did you get these, my boy?"

The boy blushed and looked down, twisting his fingers in embarrassment.

"Speak up, Tripp," said the landlord sternly. "Answer the gentleman, and see that you tell the truth."

"I ain't going to tell no lie," said Tripp doggedly. "I found this here bottle in the bureau-drawer of number fourteen a few days ago."

"Fourteen? That's the room Mr. Willard had," said Mr. Taylor, reflectively.

"Yessir, but he didn't leave them there. They were there before. I seen 'em, and I knew that hatchet-faced hardware man left 'em; then Mr. Willard, he come, but he didn't swipe 'em, so I did. That ain't no harm, is it?"

"Not a bit," said Fleming Stone, "since you've told the truth about it, and here's a dollar for your honesty. And I'm going to ask you not to say anything more about the matter, for a few days at least. Also I'm going to ask to be allowed to take a look at room number fourteen."

"Certainly, sir. Tripp, show the gentleman up," and Mr. Taylor fairly rubbed his hands with satisfaction to think that he and his premises were being made use of by the great detective.

154

"Yessir. It's at the back of the house, sir. This way, sir."

Mr. Stone's survey of the room was exceedingly brief. He gave one glance around, looked out of the only window it contained, tried the key in the lock, and then expressed himself satisfied.

Tripp, disappointed at the quickly-finished performance, elaborately pointed out the exact spot where he had found the cachou bottle, but Mr. Stone did not seem greatly interested.

However, the interview was financially successful to Tripp, and after Mr. Stone's departure he turned several hand-springs by way of expressing his satisfaction with the detective gentleman.

After dinner that evening the group of the night before reassembled in the library.

A strange feeling of oppression seemed to hang over all. The very fact that Fleming Stone had as yet said nothing of any discoveries he might have made, and the continued courtesy of his pleasant, affable demeanor, seemed to imply that he had succeeded rather than failed in his mission.

Although genial and quickly responsive, he was, after all, an inscrutable man; and Mr. Fairbanks, for one, had learned that his gentle cordiality often hid deep thoughts in a quickly-working mind.

Without preamble, as soon as they were seated Mr. Stone began:

"Employed by Coroner Benson, I was asked to come here to discover, if might be, the murderer of Miss Madeleine Van Norman. By some unmistakable evidence which I have found, by some reliable witnesses with whom I have talked, and by some proofs which I have discovered, I have learned beyond all doubt who is the criminal, and how the deed was done. Is it the wish of all present that I should now make known what I have discovered, or is it preferred that I should tell Coroner Benson alone?"

For several minutes nobody spoke, and then the coroner said, "Unless any one present states an objection, you may proceed to tell us what you know, here and now, Mr. Stone."

After waiting a moment longer and hearing no objection raised, Fleming Stone proceeded.

"The man who murdered Miss Van Norman entered the house through a cellar window. He climbed up through the ash-chute in the drawing-room fireplace."

Although some of Mr. Stone's hearers had listened to this revelation in the morning, the others had not heard of it, and every face expressed utter astonishment, if not unbelief—with the exception of one. Tom Willard turned white and stared at Fleming Stone as if he had not understood.

"What?" he said hoarsely.

155

As if he had not heard the interruption, Fleming Stone went on: "Who that man was, I think I need not tell you. Is he not already telling you himself?"

Willard's face grew drawn and stiff, like that of a paralyzed man, but his burning eyes seemed unable to tear themselves away from the quiet gaze of Fleming Stone. Then with a groan Willard's head sank into his hands and he fell forward on the table—the very table at which Madeleine had sat on that fatal night.

There was a stir, and Schuyler Carleton rushed forward to Willard's assistance if need be. But the man had not fainted, and, raising his white face, he squared his shoulders, clenched his hands, and, again fixing his eyes on those of Fleming Stone, said in a desperate voice, "Go on."

"I must go on," said Stone, gently. "I know each one of you is thinking that it is absurd to imagine a man of Mr. Willard's weight and girth climbing up through the seemingly small opening in the fireplace. But this can be explained. To one who does not know how, such a feat would seem impossible, and, moreover, it would be impossible. It is only one who knows how who can do it. There are men in certain occupations, such as engineers and boiler men, who are continually obliged to squeeze through holes quite as small. The regular boiler man-hole is oval, and measures ten by fifteen inches, but there are many of them in large tanks which measure even less each way. I had occasion some time ago to interview an engineer on this subject. He weighed two hundred and fifteen pounds, and had a chest measure of forty-two inches. He told me that he could go through a much smaller man-hole than another workman who weighed only one hundred and sixty pounds, simply because he knew how. It is done by certain manipulations of the great muscles and by following a certain routine of procedure. But the method is unimportant, for the moment. The fact remains, and can be verified by any engineer. I discovered to-day that Mr. Willard is or has been an expert engineer, and for many years held such a position in a large factory right here in Mapleton. As to Mr. Willard's presence in this house upon that fatal night, a tiny clue discovered by Mr. Fessenden gives us indubitable proof. Mr. Fessenden found next morning on the drawing-room floor a cachou. I have learned that these are by no means in common use in Mapleton, and, moreover, that it is not the custom of any one of the men now present to use them. I further learned that after Mr. Willard left here that night to go to the hotel he found by chance a small bottle of these in the room which was assigned to him. I am assuming that he carelessly put a few in his pocket, and that in his struggle through the ash-chute one fell upon the carpet. The room which Mr. Willard

156

occupied at Mapleton Inn is in the second story, and its window opens upon a veranda roof which has a gentle slope almost to the ground. This provides an easy means of exit and entrance, and as Mr. Willard has no alibi later than half-past ten on that evening, the time would permit him to come here and go away again before the hour when Mr. Carleton is known to have arrived."

Then turning and meeting Tom's intent gaze, Fleming Stone addressed himself directly to him, and said, "Why you chose to kill your cousin, I don't know; but you did."

"I did," said Tom, in a hollow voice, "and I will tell you why." He rose as he spoke, and standing by the table, he steadied himself by placing one hand upon it.

"It was entirely unpremeditated," he said, "and I'm going to tell you about it, because I owe a confession to Madeleine's memory, though I am responsible for my deed to no one here present."

Though Willard spoke with no attempt at pride or defiance, his tone and look were those of a man hopeless and utterly crushed. He addressed himself principally to Fleming Stone, looking now and then at Carleton, but not so much as glancing at any one else.

"It is no secret, I think, that I loved my cousin Madeleine. Many, many times I have pleaded with her to marry me. But never mind about that. When I came here to attend her wedding, I couldn't help seeing that the man she was about to marry did not love and worship her as I did. I besought her to give him up and to marry me, but she would not listen to that for a moment. That day before the wedding they had a little tiff, and Carleton did not return for dinner, though Madeleine expected him. She was all broken up about this, and was not herself during the evening. When I left her, at about ten o'clock, to go to the hotel, her sad face haunted me, and I could not dispel the idea that I must have one more talk with her, and beg her not to marry a man who did not love her."

Without seeming to do so, Fleming Stone stole a glance at Carleton. The man sat quietly, with bowed head, as one who hears himself denounced, but recognizes the truth.

"I was in my room at the hotel," went on Tom, "and was preparing for bed when the irresistible impulse came to me to go and see Maddy once more before her wedding day. I had no thought of wrong-doing. I came out through the window, instead of in the ordinary way, only because I knew the inn was about to be closed for the night, and I knew I could get back the same way. A trellis, that was simply a ladder, reached up to the low roof, and it was quite as easy an exit as through the front door. As to the cachous, I had found the stray vial there, and had slipped a couple in my pocket, without really thinking anything about it. I don't usually

157

carry them, but they are by no means unfamiliar to me. I came directly over here, and found the house partially darkened, as if for the night. There was a low light in the library and hall but the blinds were drawn, and I could see only a glimpse of Maddy's yellow dress on the floor. I was about to ring the bell, when I suddenly thought that I didn't care to rouse the household, or even the servants, and, remembering the way I often used to get in when I came home at night later than my uncle approved, I went around and entered by a cellar window. I came up through the fireplace, exactly as Mr. Stone has described to you. It is astonishingly easy to any one who knows how, and quite impossible for one who does not. I crossed the drawing-room at once, and entered the library. Naturally, I made very little noise, but still I am surprised that Hunt did not hear me. I did not try to be entirely silent, for I had no thought of evil in my heart. Madeleine looked up as I came into this room, and smiled. She asked me how I got in, and I told her, and we both laughed at some old reminiscences. I did not see that paper that Miss Dupuy wrote. Then I told her frankly that I wanted her to give up Carleton, for he did not love her and I did. When I said that about Carleton, Maddy burst into weeping, and said it wasn't true. I said it was, and offered to prove it, and then we quarrelled. To you who do not know our family temper this may sound trivial, but it was not. We had a most intense and fiery quarrel, and though probably our voices were not raised—that was not our way—we were so furious with each other that we were practically beside ourselves. Maddened, too, by jealousy, and by being baffled in my errand, I suddenly resolved to kill both my cousin and myself. I picked up the dagger and told her what I was about to do, being fully determined to stab her and then myself. She did not scream, she simply sat there—in her superb beauty—her arm resting on the table, and said quietly, 'You dare not do it!'

"This threw me into a frenzy, and with one thrust I drove the dagger home to her heart. She died without a sound, and I pulled out the dagger to turn it upon myself. But the sight of Madeleine's blood brought me to my senses. I dropped the dagger and new thoughts came rushing to my mind thick and fast. Madeleine was dead. I could not bring her again to life. The fortune was now mine! Would I not be a fool then to kill myself? I'm not excusing these thoughts; I'm simply telling the thing as it occurred. I turned and softly recrossed the hall, let myself down through the drawing-room fireplace, and was back in my room at the hotel without having met any one going or coming. At two o'clock I was summoned over here by telephone, and I came. Miss Morton met me in the parlor, and as there was a bright light there then, I chanced to see one of those miserable cachous on the carpet. I picked it up and concealed it, but it warned me; and when Mr. Fessenden asked me the next day if I had any, I said no. Now I have told you all. Wait—do not speak! I know you would say that I was a coward not to take my own life when I intended to. I admit it; I was a coward, but it is not yet too late for the deed!"

Before any one could move to prevent it Tom had grasped the dagger from the drawer where it was hidden and plunged it into his own breast. He sank down into the chair—the very chair where Madeleine had died, and, dreadful as the occasion was, those who saw him could not but feel that it was just retribution.

It was Schuyler Carleton who again started forward, and put his arm around the wounded man.

"Tom," he cried, "oh, Tom, why did you do that?" Carleton then involuntarily started to pull the dagger away, but Tom stopped him.

"Don't," he said thickly. "To pull that out will finish me. Leave it, and I have a few moments more!"

"That is true," said Fleming Stone. "Some one telephone for a doctor, but do not disturb the weapon. Mr. Willard, if you have anything to say, say it quickly."

"I will," said Tom, quickly; "Fessenden, you are a lawyer, will you draw up my will?"

Without a word, Rob caught up paper and pen, and prepared to take the last words of the dying man.

Though not entirely in legal phrasing, the will was completed, and after a general bequest to Fessenden himself, and directing that all bills should be paid, and other minor matters of the sort, Tom Willard left the bulk of his fortune to Schuyler Carleton.

"That," he said, with almost his last breath, "is only a deed of justice, in the name of Madeleine and myself."

Before the arrival of Doctor Hills, Tom Willard was dead. Self-confessed, self-convicted, self-punished; but his crime was discovered by Fleming Stone, and proved by means of a tiny clue.

Printed in the USA
CPSIA information can be obtained
at www.ICGtesting.com
LVHW030003300723
753626LV00018B/430/J